BOUNTY OF THE BAY

Printed in the United States of America
First Printing, 2015

ISBN 978-0-9963375-0-2

Old Mount Vernon Publishing House
Alexandria, Virginia

Illustrations by Michael Dougherty.
Designed by Josef Beery.

Bounty of the Bay

A TREASURY OF FOODS FROM THE TIDEWATERS OF THE CHESAPEAKE BAY

COMPILED BY THE LADIES OF THE WATTS ISLAND GOURMANDS SOCIETY

MICHAEL DOUGHERTY
EDITOR

From the Editor

The contents of this little book on foods from the tidewater region of the Chesapeake Bay were apparently gathered by the ladies of the Watts Island Gourmands Society between the 1930s and 1950s.

Two years ago, the last surviving member of the Society shared with me a worn, mimeographed copy of the text, asking that I edit it and perhaps have it published. She has since passed on.

Having spent some time with the document, I must admit having problems authenticating numerous events and persons described here: some are supported by the historical record, many others are not, and some simply contradict it. For these reasons, this book should be regarded as a work of fiction. As a service to the reader, I have included some brief historical notes and other comments at the end of the book.

Another caution that I would share with you is this: on no account should the reader attempt any of the recipes in this book, as they are likely to make you very ill.

Michael Dougherty
Alexandria, Virginia
March 2015

Contents

Smith Island 21-Layer German Chocolate Cake

The quiet, congenial manners common to those who dwell in the Tidewater Region should not be mistaken for passivity or slowness of mind. Many leaders, thinkers, heroes and active men of the cloth and of commerce have originated here. Indeed, it is hard to find some little byway, creek or cove that does not have its star, and often more than one.

Likewise, the civility of local folk should not be mistaken for virtue in every case. While great vices struggle to find a toehold here, there is more than enough folly, vanity and pure foolishness to go around. And, when one combines youth, beauty, pride, an impossible naiveté and skilled baking with a desperate group of German sailors in wartime, the mixture can result in something that comes very close to what we might call treason.

🍂   🍂   🍂

Our tale starts with two young ladies—for the sake of discretion, we will call them Burnetta and Tabitha

Parker—who lived in Hacksneck, Virginia. Hacksneck is a thumb of land that extends a little way into the Chesapeake Bay from Virginia's Eastern Shore. It is bounded on the north side by Butcher Creek and on the south by Nandua Creek, both navigable by small craft. To the south and west are low marshes fringed by pleasant white sand beaches that face the Bay.

Burnetta and Tabitha were cousins. They lived on adjoining farms on Nandua Creek. Each farm had its own rambling house, weathered barns, and dock extending well out to deep water. The girls were unstudied, classic beauties. Burnetta had lustrous raven hair and dark blue eyes, while Tabitha was blond and green-eyed. Each was athletic but pleasingly shaped, with the healthy complexions that come to those who work in fresh air charged by gusts off the open Atlantic and the lower Bay.

Hacksneck is a remote place. To get there from Route 13, one has to pass through Coocheyville and Pungoteague over a series of macadam roads that twist and turn along ancient property lines, natural hazards, and through several forests of loblolly pine. Lightly populated at any time, Hacksneck was even more deserted in the spring of 1945, when men were away on wartime service and women were employed in distant locales like the Martin plant up in Middle River, building bombers to crush our totalitarian foes.

Burnetta and Tabitha were rising seniors at Central High School, too young to be formally employed in the war effort. When not in school, they were busy contributing to the work about their families' rich farms. Nearly anything will grow in the soil of Hacksneck, and in their proper order apricots, blueberries, plums, peaches, and apples were packed and shipped away. For local consumption there were beans, blackberries, carrots, broccoli, cherries, sweet corn, melons, tomatoes, peppers and pumpkins, as well as raspberries and cucumbers.

Raised from childhood in close proximity, Burnetta and Tabitha were more sisters than cousins, and amicable companions in most every way. Their friendship, however, ended at the doorway to the kitchen. An unusual rivalry had first manifested itself at the age of seven, when they were decorating cookies on Christmas Eve. The girls were heard to disagree about the merits of green sprinkles over jimmies. After a long unnatural silence, they suddenly flew at one another in a clawing fight that began in the kitchen and ended in the yard. The girls' stunned parents sent them crying to bed without dinner; their older brothers, who seldom missed the opportunity for a laugh at their expense, showed a tact rare in boys and never mentioned the event again.

There was no more open brawling between Burnetta and Tabitha. It was replaced with a smoldering conflict, a kind of peripheral border war where neither side could gain the ascendancy, but peeked now and again over the trench tops to check the enemy's progress and returned to its own tunneling, seeking to place the fatal mine and win the field.

As war sees the perfection of every device and tactic meant to defeat the opponent, so the girls grew in the baking arts, turning out peach layer cakes, molasses pecan pies, custards, puddings, carnival cakes and fruit tortes of every variety with a cold skill. An apple, blueberry or cherry pie, bubbling and piping under a perfectly browned lattice of flaky crust and drowned in clotted cream, would be thoughtlessly created between homework and dinner, while reading a book. Breads, muffins and buns—thrown away beauty left to cool on the windowsill—would bring dogs and moonstruck farm hands nearly breaking into a trot.

As is usual in war, it was not the combatants who profited so much as those on the periphery, like men at the country fair who enjoyed white cake drooping heavy with butter cream frosting; or boys at bond drives who gobbled up dozens of penny buns with glasses of milk; or circling housewives at church bazaars who wanted the latest intelligence on the girl's recipes.

       🞰   🞰   🞰

The Second World War might be raging in Europe and the Pacific, but there was no war to be found on the Chesapeake Bay. The lack of action rankled some of the younger crew on board the *Yippe 489* (Navy YP 489), but it perfectly suited the yard patrol boat's captain, an insouciant Philadelphia lawyer who was 4-F'd from more dangerous theaters of operation. On this mild May afternoon in 1945, it was obvious to anyone who bothered to read the latest edition of *Stars and Stripes* that the war in Germany was as good as over, and that the Japanese were near done, as fleets of Superfortresses were turning Tokyo into a smoldering ruin. The captain was fine with whatever duty the Navy assigned his converted wooden shrimp trawler, up from the Louisiana coast and still smelling of overripe shellfish under her grey paint. The 489 was outfitted for anti-submarine operations with a rack of depth charges, a 3-inch gun, two mounted .50 caliber machine guns, and a small armory of personal weapons.

It was always surprising to the captain how little escaped the notice of the 489's standing watch, composed of several determined young men with powerful marine binoculars and nothing to do but look through them. Patrolling up the shoreline from Cape Charles, they had spotted porpoises that might be torpedoes, the head of a big leatherback turtle that might be a periscope, and even a lone whale that was almost certainly a submarine. The captain forbid them from making war on any of these creatures.

As the 489 approached the mouth of Nandua Creek, the captain was again called topside by the watch.

"What's up?" he asked.

"Thirty degrees, Captain. You see the long dock with the workboat tied up to it?"

"Yes."

"There's a girl on the dock." The remainder of the watch wandered over to have a look.

"Wow, that's a nice looking dame," said someone.

"Yeah, but she's giving that fellow on the workboat a couple of packages," said one of the watch. "It looks suspicious, Captain, maybe we should investigate!"

The captain had no interest in pretty girls—as the

father of three of his own, he had come to regard females of any age as simply charming, troublesome beings from another planet—but thought the crew was ready for a break in the monotony of this *pro forma* patrol.

"What's the chart say?"

"Six feet mean low water. We got that and a lunar flood."

"Take it slow. I don't want to get stuck. Set throttle at low maneuver."

As the *489* edged into Nandua Creek, the workboat headed out in the opposite direction, a neat stack of crab traps arranged along her afterdeck. The workboat's mate was observed opening one of two square pink boxes on the flat of the engine hood, sawing away with a fighting knife, and pulling forth a fat slice of black and yellow cake, which he examined at eye level as though it were a jewel of price. A smile was on his face until he noticed the *489* close aboard. As the two craft passed one another, the mate gave the *489*'s crew an impassive look with a barely perceptible nod of the head—the eternal greeting that watermen give to people they don't know, and the same they give to St. Peter on entering heaven.

꧁ ꧁ ꧁

Tabitha remained standing on her family's long wooden dock, folding the waterman's dollar bills into her jeans pocket as the *489* carefully edged to a stop and threw a line over the bollard.

Smoke from the patrol boat's maneuvering had summoned Ted Twombly, an old field hand, to the water's edge. He rolled a cigarette and watched as Tabitha spoke with the white-hatted captain. After a brief exchange, the *489* cast off and three pairs of binoculars rose in unison to follow Tabitha's progress down the dock. Ted frowned. He heard a faint cry of "eyes in the boat!" from the *Yippe*'s captain, and the *489* chugged off to continue her patrol.

"What was that all about, miss?"

"Hello, Ted! More customers for my Smith Island cake! They want three by tomorrow afternoon—imagine, that will be six whole dollars!"

"Hmm. I'm not sure that your father would approve of you selling cakes to Navy men, miss."

Tabitha laughed. "Well, Ted, you can be my protector tomorrow when I hand over the goods. Six dollars!"

Burnetta meanwhile was tending her farm's two Jersey cows (the soft roan beauties turned out an extraordinary high fat milk so delicious in butter and cheeses). She was not known for spying, but the oversized cloud of diesel smoke emanating from the *Yippe*'s stacks drew her down to the water, where she was screened by a weeping willow that marked the property line between the Parker farms. She was astonished to see so large a craft in their little creek, and equally astonished to see Tabitha conversing so casually with the captain of what could only be described as a warship. Fragments of their conversation drifted down to her. She distinctly heard the words *Smith*, *cake* and *dollars*.

Her color rising, Burnetta came to a sudden realization:

Tabitha was running a Smith Island Cake trade right off her own back yard! The audacity of it stunned her. Boat traffic from oystermen, crabbers and fisherman to her cousin's dock had increased in recent weeks, but Burnetta had scarce paid any attention—now she understood. If memory served her, those work boats looked to be coming from nearby Tangier's Island and from Smith Island itself—deadrises with names like the *Miss Susie*, the *Melanie Ann*, *Nautical Nonsense*, and the *Captain Chappy*. If the women from those venerable low islands had any idea that their men folk were actually *buying Smith Island Cake from an off-islander*! Those fellows would not be hearing the word "*Hon*" spoken to them for a long time!

Burnetta finished her work in the yard, and then walked into the kitchen. As she washed her hands in the sink, she had an old thought come into her head. It was not a good thought, and she had pushed it away many times in the past, but now she found herself nodding, her mouth a grim line. It could be done now. Burnetta dried her hands, pulled a fresh apron over her head, and tied it close. She opened the cupboard. There, gleaming in the half light, were tidy rows of gunmetal cake pans. She would make a Smith Island Cake such as had never been seen before.

❦   ❦   ❦

Dear reader, you may look throughout this narrative for a Smith Island Cake recipe, but you will not find one here. One does not need to know how to make them—we leave the baking of these cakes to the women of Smith

Island, who first created them, perfected them, and claim proper ownership over them. We *purchase* our Smith Island Cake *from* Smith Island.

That said, we may briefly describe this Tidewater treasure. In its classic form, the cake itself is round and yellow. There are between seven and twelve layers of cake. These layers are cut thin and even. The "frosting" is not really a frosting at all, but more a dark chocolate fudge. The fudge better maintains moisture within the cake, keeping it fresh longer. It is also more durable—when a waterman is out of port for two weeks dredging oysters in ice-cold, three-foot-high waves, and pulls his gloves off for a snack, he does not want his cake coming apart in his hand. And, if the world is right, that waterman is thinking about the sweetheart who baked it as he enjoys its wholesome goodness.

Some variation of the Smith Island Cake is tolerated. There are coconut, peanut-butter, red velvet and lemon crème versions, to be sure, but on the whole, one does not *show away* with a cake style that has hundreds of years of tradition behind it.

≈≈≈   ≈≈≈   ≈≈≈

As Burnetta arranged her cake pans and began furiously lashing ingredients together, two secretive visitors were burrowed deep into the mud and muck of the marsh along Nandua Creek opposite the Parker farms. They were *Oberleutnant zur See* Hans-Joachim Schwarz and *Leitender Ingenieur* Rudi Van de Mal of the German *Kriegsmarine*. Schwarz was the commander of

Unterseeboot 1105, and Van de Mal her lead engineer. Like most U-boaters, they were young. At age 25, Schwarz was the oldest man on the boat. Van de Mal was only 23. Draped in camouflage smocks, they watched as the *489* made the Bay, turned north and smoked out of sight.

The German's U-boat lay two miles away, submerged in 60 feet of water on the bottom of the Chesapeake. The *Yippe* had already twice passed directly over the 1105, pinging away with her sonar, but did not detect the submarine. That was by design: the 1105 was a very special kind of Type VII-C boat, featuring an experimental technology known by the codename *Alberich*, a reference to the dwarf in Wagner's mythic *Ring Cycle* operas, who steals gold from three vain water nymphs to fashion a ring of power. *Alberich* was a synthetic rubber skin composed of hundreds of anechoic tiles that wrapped the hull of the 1105, absorbing and diffusing the sound waves produced by active sonar and making it practically invisible to Allied surface ships. The 38-man crew called their submarine, *The Black Panther*, and the conning tower of  their boat sported a snarling cat draped over the globe.

❧   ❧   ❧

Schwarz and Van de Mal were physically and emotionally drained. In the second week of April, the *Black Panther* had received a terse order from U-boat headquarters (*Befehlshaber der Unterseeboote*, or B.d.U.) in Berlin: "Proceed at highest safe speed and without engaging enemy forces to Yankee Station in preparation for attack on Washington, D.C. Do not operate radios, repeat, maintain strict radio silence in transit. Contact B.d.U by KURIER flash transmission on arrival at Yankee Station for additional orders."

The *Black Panther* dashed across the Atlantic, surfacing for high speed runs at night, deploying its *schnorchel* in low-light conditions and moderate swells to stay on the faster diesel engines, and operating on the slow but silent electric motors when Allied warships lay across her path. The Atlantic was an Allied lake—the U-boat encountered so many Royal Navy, Canadian and U.S destroyers and escorts that her crew swore they could hopscotch across them to the American shore. They made at least a dozen crash-dives at night, when four-engined bombers suddenly appeared against the stars, seeking prey. The men waited breathlessly in the gloom of battle lamps for the depth bombs that would split the U-boat's hull and send her on an uncontrolled dive to oblivion. But the magic of *Alberich* kept them safe.

The submarine made Yankee Station—the 20-fathom mark off the entrance to Chesapeake Bay—just after dark on Tuesday, May 1. The air inside the boat was close and humid as she crept along the seafloor on her e-motors. There were fast ships moving in every direction overhead, and the swish of their screws beating the water was dimly heard and felt through the *Alberich* hull. Schwarz waited a couple of hours until the traffic quieted down, and then ordered the *Black Panther* off the bottom.

In the 1105's control room, Schwarz turned to the

funkmaat (radioman). "Be ready with the KURIER flash, we want to be up and down as fast as possible." *You just never know,* he thought, *there might be an American destroyer loitering on the surface with her engines off and sound gear on.*

The KURIER system would send a burst signal lasting only 452 milliseconds to a B.d.U receiving station, but it was a one-way, outbound transmission that would do nothing more than tell B.d.U that they were here. And, it would take hours for B.d.U to decode. *Black Panther* would have to use her standard *Telefunken* VLF receiver to get further orders for the attack on Washington, which meant that she would need to remain on the surface, or close to it, and be exposed to detection in one of the busiest shipping lanes in the world.

"Periscope depth!"

With the U-boat hovering 17 feet below the surface, Schwarz peered rapidly in every direction through the navigation 'scope. Seeing nothing, he ordered the boat up. As the 1105's conning tower broke the surface, the radioman touched the signal key to launch the KURIER message. With that, all hell broke loose. Several loud bangs behind the radio panel were followed by a great blinding flash and a billowing wave of acrid smoke.

"Dive!"

Working through the dense smoke, Van de Mal and the radioman at first thought the high humidity in the boat had shorted the KURIER's delicate KGZ 44/2 pulse generator. "These *Geber's* are delicate babies, Captain," said the engineer, "they don't like the wet." But, as they pulled the front panel off the transmission set, they found blast marks and paper wrapping among the scorched and torn wires.

"It must be sabotage," said Van del Mal slowly. "Some clever Bolshevik rigged squibs across the entire communications system. He's fried the KURIER and both sets of transmitters and receivers. It's a complicated job, but cheap. It would have been done when we were fitting out at the boat yard in Wilhelmshaven."

"Can you fix it?" asked Schwarz.

"No. Not with what we have on the boat."

"Well, we can't hang around here. Let's go into the Chesapeake."

After ghosting past Cape Charles in the wake of a northbound freighter, Schwarz looked over the charts with Van de Mal and his first watch officer. "Where can we get a high-frequency radio—aside from asking the U.S. Navy to give us one?"

The first watch officer raised a finger. "A farm. Farmers like to tinker—natural radio buffs, some of them. A rural farm, I should think. I'll wager we can find one or two here," he said, lowering his finger to the chart of the Virginia Eastern Shore. "All we need to do is look for the little HAM towers."

In the predawn hours of Wednesday, May 2, Schwarz and Van de Mal left the 1105 in an inflatable raft and paddled stealthily into Nandua Creek, where they set up their observation post. At present, they were extremely uncomfortable. While the sun had shined on them all day, it was only 55 degrees and the peat of the marsh was soggy with water, while the grey mud underneath gave off a distinctive odor. The low brown stalks of last year's sea oats stabbed their hands and knees. They had lain on their bellies for hours, watching the comings and goings on the Parker farms. The *Yippe*'s trip into the creek had frightened them—they thought they were discovered—but when they realized the trawler only wanted to talk to the pretty blond, they simply nodded to one another: navy boys were the same all over the world.

The thing that fixed their attention was a decrepit radio tower sticking skyward from a large, sunburned red barn. They watched as a dark-haired girl led two cows into the barn, and then emerged to walk into a white frame farmhouse.

Van de Mal shifted on his elbows to get a clearer view through the grass. "Captain," he whispered, "we've been on three cruises together and I can tell you frankly that I don't think much of this plan."

"It's not a bad plan, Rudi. We just wait until it gets a little darker, we paddle the raft over to that dock, find the radio attached to that aerial, liberate it and carry it back to the *Panther*."

"I mean the mission. How is the *Panther* going to attack the city of Washington? It's a political stunt dreamed up by some fool at B.d.U. No military value."

"Now, now, Rudi. Orders are orders."

"Captain. If we even make it up the Potomac, every Yank in sight will start shooting our asses out of the water the moment we light up our deck gun."

Schwarz let it pass, and the two men lapsed into silence.

All afternoon, V formations of Canada geese had passed at high altitude, honking. A tight pack of ruddy ducks, flying low and heading west, winged overhead with a whistle. The water by their hide was alive with big rockfish, pushing bait against the wall of the marsh and sometimes leaving the water with a heavy splash. A pair of red-eyed canvasback ducks paddled past the commotion, and then dove from sight.

"This place is a sportsman's paradise, Captain."

"Yes, it is." The lights turned on in the kitchen of Burnetta's farm house. "It's dark enough. Let's get going."

*   *   *

Things seemed to go pretty well at first. Van de Mal disappeared into the depths of the barn with a shaded flashlight. Schwarz stood watch outside, listening to the crickets and watching bats dip and dive. He gave a guilty shrug, thinking of his men holed up in the foul air of the 1105, but it was nice to be out of that submarine for a few hours, inhaling the smell of fading peach blossoms and fresh cut grass.

As a sailor, Schwarz had seen many coastlines, some dramatic, some violent, some picturesque. This place was not so obvious. But it was very good in its quiet, mellow way, rich and ready-made for living.

Rudi was right about this mission. It was foolish and without military value. It could not have been approved by *Großadmiral* (Grand Admiral) Karl Dönitz, himself a U-boat man and pragmatic in every way. It must have originated among the B.d.U staff.

If a fool gives an order, Schwarz thought, *does it take an even greater fool to carry it out? Perhaps it does. But I am not a fool.*

Rudi returned. "There's no radio in there."

"It's probably in the house."

"What are we going to do?"

"We'll just go up to the house and ask for it. Do you speak English?"

"Not much."

"I'm fluent. Talk as little as possible and we'll get by."

Burnetta had finished baking 21 flat yellow cake layers and was working up the fudge frosting when there was a knock on the screen door. She did not welcome the distraction—putting all of this together was going to be difficult.

Burnetta assumed from Schwarz's peaked white hat that he was the captain of the *Yippe,* but thought the pair standing on the porch were the most disheveled Navy men she'd ever seen, bearded, wearing grey leather coats, thick turtleneck sweaters and smelling of diesel fumes and Bay mud.

"Yes?"

"Good evening. We have come to ask for the loan of your HAM radio. Ours has broken and we need to talk to headquarters."

"Oh. That old radio of Dad's is broken."

"I am sure that we can make it work. Perhaps we can even fix it for him."

"That would be nice. How long would you have it?"

"A couple of days only. We will bring it back."

"Ok. It's in the barn inside a couple of cardboard boxes on the front seat of the old truck." Van de Mal Rudi kicked himself—he'd passed by the Ford Model A pickup, its windows covered with a thick layer of dust. "Do you need me to show you?" she asked.

"No. We will find it."

"Alright then. By the way, did you order a Smith Island Cake from my cousin Tabitha today?"

Schwarz was at a loss but recovered quickly—clearly, she thought he was someone else, and that was good. "Yes, I did," he lied. He had no idea what a Smith Island Cake was, but it was obvious that the young lady was baking—a delicious smell of cake was wafting through the screen door.

"How many layers is Tabitha going to put on it for you? The usual seven?"

"Yes, seven seems good."

"I can do it better than that."

"You can?"

"Yes, the Smith Island Cake I'm baking now is going to have 21 layers!"

"That's remarkable! May we come in and see your work?"

She lead Schwarz and Van de Mal into the kitchen. There were pans holding thin golden cakes cooling all over the counters and dinner table.

Schwarz inhaled deeply, his arms crossed behind his

back. "Your cooking is sublime, miss!" he said with a broad smile. This was no amateur. There was a discipline here that he immediately respected. He gestured towards a big ceramic bowl on the counter. "That looks like 3 whole liters, uh, a half gallon of frosting!"

"It's a lot—I've never made a cake this big."

"Well, miss, if you are looking to be innovative, you could make the frosting more interesting by adding coconut and crushed pecans to the mix."

"You mean German chocolate frosting?" asked Burnetta dubiously, "on a Smith Island cake?"

She thought for a second. She was already over the fence and running wild on this caper, breaking conventions, breaking faith with a creed that did not even have a name . . . yes it did, it was called tradition and tradition was sacred. But there were times to step out. These two Navy men looked gaunt, tired and somehow foreign in the light of the kitchen. She pitied them.

"Well, I can do it if you all are looking to buy this cake."

"We would be delighted to buy the cake, except it would need to be on credit—I am afraid that we have no cash."

"You can pay me when you bring the radio back?"

"Yes, and if you will allow me, I will leave you this memento as security on the debt," Schwarz said, holding out a large enamel pin that featured the *Black Panther* logo. It was an expensive birthday gift from his crew. The snarling black cat had diamond stud eyes and sat on a globe of 18-carat gold. He almost checked himself, but Burnetta's movie-star looks, the warm fragrant domesticity of the kitchen, the weeks of unending pressure and the threat of tomorrow, all did their work on him. *If I am still in this world when the war is over*, he thought, *I will come back and get my pin.*

"My goodness," said Burnetta admiringly as she it to pinned it to her apron. "Whatever is it?"

"It represents our boat and the men who serve on it."

"Thank you." Suddenly all business, she said, "Well, I need to get to it. There's some coffee in the percolator from this morning if you want to heat it back up. The cake will be ready in a half hour."

Schwarz and Van de Mal made a midnight rendezvous with the *Black Panther* off Hacksneck. Their treasures were handed down through the dripping conning tower. First the radio, then a cake box, and then a 10-gallon can of milk.

"*Mein Gott*," exclaimed the first mate with a grin on his bearded face, "we must send you ashore more often, Captain!"

When they made deeper water, Schwarz ordered the 1105 to the bottom, and invited the crew towards the control room.

"Comrades," he said, "we have good news. We have a radio that the *Leitender Ingenieur* assures me can be repaired so that we can talk to Berlin." There was a low cheer. "And we also have a treat, courtesy of a very kind and beautiful American *fräulein*. Every man may have a look before we cut into this delightful confection." He pulled the cake from its box, a tall, perfect brown cylinder of a cake that gave off a rich gleam. "It is called Smith Island 21-Layer German Chocolate Cake!" The *Black Panther* device was featured on top in white frosting. The cake smelled of hearth and home. Some men wept.

🕮   🕮   🕮

The *Black Panther* spent the remainder of the night slowly spinning her propellers northwest towards the Potomac River. The radioman troubleshot the HAM radio, and then carefully dismantled it, checking for breaks or opens in the wiring. He saw where the farmer had lost his way, inserting the wrong voltage cathode bypass and even mysteriously soldering wires to the wrong leads. "*Radios are not for everyone*," he mused to himself, rummaging around in his box of spare parts. When the radio was up and humming, he began fashioning an aerial out of wire and a broom handle.

It was noon on Thursday, May 3, when the *Black Panther* passed Point Lookout at the open mouth of the Potomac, 30 feet below the surface. The sub was 96 water miles from Washington. "Let's make a few more miles," said Schwartz to the first officer. "We will surface after dark and deploy the radio. The crew should sleep—it's only going to get busier from this point."

An hour past sunset, the *Black Panther* rose slowly to periscope depth in 91 feet of water. As the navigation 'scope broke the surface, Schwarz pivoted rapidly in a circle.

"Looks good, all clear! Blow tanks slowly, I just want the tower out of the water." The watch scrambled up the conning tower, opening the dripping hatches as they went. The makeshift aerial was handed up.

In the control room, the radioman sat hunched over his work station, listening intently through his earphones for high-frequency radio traffic and alternating between the America 1, 2 and 3 circuits that B.d.U used to communicate with its boats on station near the United States, bouncing signals off the ionosphere.

The radio was silent until 9:15 p.m. ". . . *bogen*," said a hollow, deep voice through the static. Very slowly, and with great deliberation, the otherworldly voice repeated, "*Regenbogen. Regenbogen. Regenbogen.*"

"*Regenbogen*," said the radioman, wonderingly. "B.d.U. is transmitting it over and over. What could it mean?"

"Let me listen," said Schwarz, reaching for the headset and pressing it against his ear. There it was: "*Rainbow. Rainbow. Rainbow.*" Schwarz slowly lowered the headset and walked to a little safe below his bunk, and pulled out a signal book that B.d.U had issued him before the cruise. He had an idea what the *Regenbogen* transmission meant, and the signal book confirmed it. The war was over. *Regenbogen* was B.d.U's prearranged signal to all U-boat captains to immediately scuttle their submarines to avoid the dishonor of surrendering them to the Allies. The order could only have come from Grand Admiral Dönitz, who was now steering the Third Reich through its last, troubled hours.

It was the work of a few minutes for the *Black Panther*'s crew to clear the submarine and deploy life rafts stored behind the conning tower. They paddled clear, and two minutes later the scuttling charges in the boat gave a dull roar. The U-boat rose briefly in a boil of foam and then slowly dropped from sight, settling forever to the bottom of the Potomac River at 38°08'10"N, 76°33'10"W.

᪥ ᪥ ᪥

On Friday, May 4, the police station in Montross, Virginia, received a telephone call from a distressed older resident out on Route 622 by Currioman Bay. There were dozens of nude sun-bathing males wandering around on the sands of Sharktooth Island, washing their clothes and hanging them to dry in the trees, and hooting as they dove from rubber rafts in the shallows. They were plainly visible from her front window and her little grandchildren were going to be coming over for lunch—heaven help us if they should be exposed to such a sight. Was this some kind of crackpot Navy exercise? Please remove them at once.

An hour later, the *Yippe 489* came smoking up the Potomac and took custody of the *Black Panther's* crew.

᪥ ᪥ ᪥

Even after the war, the Office of Naval Intelligence had no interest in sharing with the world that one of Germany's most advanced U-boats had penetrated U.S. coastal defenses and made it into the Potomac River. So, with the concurrence of British Intelligence, Navy officials eventually fabricated an elaborate and detailed narrative around the *Black Panther's* activities in 1945, complete with bogus logs and records, fraudulent first-hand accounts, and even doctored photographs.

Briefly, the Navy's story went something like this: On April 21, 1945, the *Black Panther* boldly attacked three British destroyers off Blackrock, Ireland, sinking the HMS *Redmill* with significant loss of life. The submarine was then subjected to the longest Allied depth-charge bombardment of the war, which lasted 31 hours. Her *Alberich* tiles saved her from precise sound detection, and she eventually managed to crawl away. On May 10, following the German surrender, the *Panther* turned herself over to Allied forces at Loch Eriboll in Scotland. After a brief possession by the Royal Navy, she was towed to the United States in 1946, where acoustic experts from the U.S. Naval Research Laboratory and the Massachusetts Institute of Technology studied her rubber skin. On September 19, 1949, the Navy towed her into the Potomac River and detonated an experimental MK.6 depth charge 30 feet from her hull. Not surprisingly, she sank.

    🐟   🐟   🐟

Today, in certain local eateries on Virginia's Eastern Shore, in restaurants so small that tourists seldom find them (except when hopelessly lost on the winding, unmarked back roads), working men will finish a lunch of corn bread and cream of crab or Navy bean soup and ask the waitress, "Ya'll got any Black Panther cake today?"

2

Croaker on a Stick

The Dorset Tavern is a stolid, Georgian red brick structure that sits at the base of the hill on Dock Street in Annapolis. The Tavern excellently serves its chilled or warmed potations to happy crowds, but is haunted in two distinct ways.

It is first haunted by a legacy of mediocre food served to generations of locals and tourists. The Tavern has eternally hovered between two and three stars in anyone's rating. It is true that Washington, Franklin and Jefferson all dined here, yet they might be what we now call "business travelers," meaning weary, harassed people between meetings and making the best of what lays at hand—with the distinction that those gentlemen were passing through Annapolis on the business of the Continental Congress.

The second haunting at Dorset Tavern is the presence of a specter that appears at the first floor window nearest the Town Dock. The apparition is that of a man, wearing clothes from another age. He stares intently towards the Town Dock to the place where the ferry

boats used to tie up when running to Rock Hall, Baltimore
or points south. He is most
often encountered on sum-
mer nights, when thunder-
storms drench the flagstones
of Market Space and winds
whip the dark surface of the
Bay. Witnesses have smelled
cigar smoke on his arrival.
When he vanishes, a stack of
dirty plates may be hurled to the floor by an invisible hand.

The Dorset Tavern staff call the phantom "Ronald."
They think he lived in the 1700s.

    ❧   ❧   ❧

If it is true that spirits haunt those places where
they experienced the great exclamation point of their
lives—some trauma, frustrated ambition, or lost love—the
staff of the Dorset Tavern may be mistaken about their
ghost. He is probably Leonard Jeffro Leroy, a Marylander
from Timonium. His ambition, and his contribution to
the culinary history of the Tidewater region, reached its
high water mark and tragedy in the year 1832.

Leroy—often referred to as "Jeffro" or for unknown reasons "Leroy Leroy" in the *Maryland Gazette* of the peri-
od—was an ambitious young hostler who tended to the
horses of the Dorset Tavern's clientele. For several years,
he zealously groomed and watered his charges, removing
stones from their hooves and rubbing soothing lotions on

their cuts, scrapes and sores. Leroy laid hands on some of the finest horse flesh in the mid-Atlantic, because the Tavern was the headquarters of the Maryland Jockey Club, now at 215 years old the most venerable sporting organization in all of North America.

At that time, the Club had some 237 members, all devoted to the sport of racing horses. Some say that it is difficult for those living in the modern era of the automobile to comprehend the singularity with which horse racing occupied the American mind in the early Nineteenth Century, but one only need compare it to famous car races such as the International 500-Mile Sweepstakes held at Indianapolis, for the ingredients are the same: fast, elite, and beautiful conveyances that rocket past the crowd; the spice of danger; the opportunity to place a bet on the outcome; social mixing; and, unfortunately, the freedom to consume large quantities of cheap alcohol, such as beer.

Americans at the time referred to race courses as "*the Turf*," but did not actually run horses on the trim, undulating grass courses favored by the English. Instead, Americans favored fresh-plowed fields or skinned dirt ovals. English riders competed with one another over courses of three-quarters to one-and-a-half miles; but Americans, who looked chiefly for "*bottom*" in horses to establish pedigree and worth, rode them very, very hard. A single "heat" ranged from three to five miles, and not less than three heats were usually expected of a competitive horse and rider.

A fast colt might cost a buyer three thousand dollars, a profound sum in the era when unskilled laborer might make 12 dollars a month; in other words, a colt represented twenty years of the common man's labor. That colt in turn could bring its owner vast wealth in purses reaching ten thousand dollars on the racing circuit from Charleston to Norfolk, Tappahannock, Annapolis, Baltimore, Philadelphia, and New York.

*   *   *

To Leroy, standing ankle-deep in horse manure and living off the tips of his patrons, such sums were beyond reach. But Leroy was an enterprising young man, and spent long hours in thought as to how he might better his situation. He had witnessed the contests near Annapolis, where thousands from city and farm would circle the race course, and even encroach on it: the jockeys, often unpaid white boys or slaves, had on occasion to steer their mounts around wandering drunken yokels. The "market" was there, sure enough. What convenience might he bring to people who had plenty to drink, but little to eat?

It was during one of these reveries on a summer evening that Leroy found himself sitting at the edge of the Town Dock, dangling his legs over the water and drinking a birch beer. Along came a crooked pine-pole skiff sculled by a Bay man. The man pulled up short, reached to his feet and drew forth a casting net, which he expertly threw in a perfect circle over the water. He allowed it to sink for some distance. Giving the net a quick jerk, he hauled a dozen small flapping croaker aboard, and continued on his way, casting now again and gradually filling his baskets with the savory fish.

At that moment, Leroy conceived his "croaker on stick," which became staple fare for race-goers throughout the region, and made "Leroy Leroy" a familiar figure behind his smoking black iron barbecues.

A young croaker of six to eight-inches is prepared by gutting, chopping off both head and tail, and is lightly 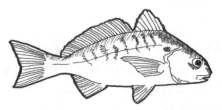 salted and peppered; a wetted wooden skewer is then driven into the body of the fish, which is grilled until brown. The fish is dipped into one of several sauces, including spicy brown mustard, honey and lemon, dill and mayonnaise, or sugared horse-radish, and eaten directly off the skewer.

In late June of 1832, Leroy set up near Snedeker's on the Jamaica Plank Road in Brooklyn, New York. Thousands of race fans heading to the Union Course were streaming by, many hoping to see paraded two of the fastest thorough-breds of the early Republic, Sir Charles from Virginia, and American Eclipse from New York, who had last met on the track a decade before and were now out to stud, but whose muscled, ribboned flanks still drew admiring crowds.

To create his sauces, Leroy drew several gallons of water from a nearby hand pump. Business was brisk: by his own account, Leroy had served some 400 customers by one o'clock in the afternoon, each carrying away a croaker and a small paper cup holding their sauce of choice.

An hour or so later, a pale-looking man stopped by and claimed Leroy's fish had made him sick. Leroy offered an apology and returned the man his five cents. Then, with alarming suddenness, the man doubled over and became violently ill. He was not alone in his distemper, for at that point in time, several other spectators at the Union Course dropped to the ground and began to vomit while completely losing control of their bowels to a vile, watery flatulence.

Cholera had come to New York City. By the time the epidemic had run its course, some 3,500 people were dead, and half the City's wealthier population was taking refuge in the hills. Learned civic leaders agreed that the affliction "is almost exclusively confined to the lower classes of intemperate dissolute & filthy people huddled together like swine in their polluted habitations," and reflected "[t]hose sickened must be cured or die off, & being chiefly of the very scum of the city, the quicker [their] dispatch the sooner the malady will cease."

Fairly or not, the racing public believed that Leroy's fish sauce was somehow to blame for the onset of the disaster. His trade having disappeared, Leroy left the Eastern Shore that fall on a three-master for San Francisco, which was said to have been lost in an early gale off Cape Horn.

For those with rod and reel, the Town Dock within sight of the southeast window of the Dorset Tavern remains a fine place to catch summer croaker.

3

Hog Island Pork Tenderloins with Fig and Rye Whisky Sauce

In attempting a rescue the keeper will select either the boat, breeches buoy, or life car. . . . If the device first selected fails . . . he will resort to one of the others, and if that fails, then to the remaining one, and he will not desist from his efforts until by actual trial the impossibility of effecting a rescue is demonstrated. The statement of the keeper that he did not try to use the boat because the sea or surf was too heavy will not be accepted unless attempts to launch it were actually made and failed. . . .

REGULATIONS OF THE LIFE-SAVING SERVICE OF 1899, ARTICLE VI, ACTION AT WRECKS, SEC. 252.

[O]ne of the men shouted out that we might make it out to the wreck but we would never make it back. The old skipper looked around and said, 'The Blue Book says we've got to go out and

*it doesn't say a damn thing about having to
come back.'*

CREDITED TO KEEPER PATRICK ETHERIDGE OF THE
CAPE HATTERAS LIFE SAVING STATION BY U.S. COAST
GUARD CHIEF BOATSWAIN'S MATE CLARENCE P. BRADY,
COAST GUARD MAGAZINE, 1954.

Summer, 1923

The men of the Prohibition Unit did not care for Southern Maryland. Driving along Route 5 was okay, but when
you left the main drag for the quiet country roads of St.
Mary's County, it was positively creepy—nothing but
fields and farm animals and pine trees and unhelpful
locals who had no idea who might be making illegal rye
whiskey. Hell, even the local lawmen, who were supposed to be helping the Prohibition Unit enforce the Volstead Act—which made it unlawful to manufacture, sell
or transport liquor—even those fellows were mum, for-
getful, late or absent altogether when it came to taking
down a moonshiner's still in their jurisdiction. It didn't
matter that moonshiners down here were patriotic, mild-
mannered, church-going farm folk whose ancestors had
brewed the stuff since the 1600s—no, what mattered
to the men of the Prohibition Unit, as sworn Federal
officers, was that *booze was now illegal.*

Angela Doughty knew that the Prohibition Unit had
taken to running joint operations with the Coast Guard
in little speedboats along the maritime borders of St.
Mary's County. She guessed they would come off the
Potomac River into Poplar Hill Creek at the southern end

of her farm, sneaking along at low speed, making a landing in the marsh by the woods and then suddenly appearing on the back lawn. That's why in recent weeks she'd stationed her German shepherds, Joey and Kaya, down on the waterfront. They were exquisitely trained as silent scouts by a WWI veteran, and would noiselessly come up to the house to alert her if any strangers entered the property.

Her wall telephone rang. She picked up the receiver.

"Good morning, Angela." It was Bernadette, the Leonardtown switchboard operator.

"Hello Bee."

"Word is that the Coast Guard picked up some Revenuers at the dock here in town. They headed out for the river. I'm calling everyone."

"How many are there?"

"Two Coasties and two Revenuers."

"Who are the Coasties?"

"Never seen them before. I hear they're bringing crews over from Virginia or elsewhere 'cause the Maryland boys don't want to arrest their friends and relations." Bee laughed. "I'll call again if I learn more."

Angela thanked her and hung up.

Angela's neighbors were hosting a potluck supper that night, and she was planning on making a big dish of paella as her share. She had a black iron skillet leaning against the wall in her kitchen. It was thirty inches across and weighed 22 pounds, and it covered all four burners of her Hotpoint electric range. It was a bit of salvage: her father had found it cast up on shore near the site of an old shipwreck, and assumed that was used to feed the crew of a coastal trading vessel, perhaps four to six men. Angela hefted the skillet onto the range, turned the burners on low, and poured on some vegetable oil to get things started. She chopped onions, carrots, celery and garlic, browned them and then added a cup of apple juice and some spicy brown mustard.

Angela could not cook paella without thinking about her mother, who was a native of Spain and a virtuoso in the dishes of her homeland. "What is paella, anyway?" she would say in her lilting voice. "It is a concoction of anything and everything good to eat. Like all great food it has humble origins. In Valencia in olden days it was used to feed field hands at the harvest, in the open and over a fire. They cooked what they had—there was always rice and some kind of vegetable, because they are clever farmers in Valencia—but for meat it was catch as catch can. Maybe they had chicken one day, maybe they had rabbit the next, maybe all they had were little green frogs out of the rice paddies!"

Angela had center cut pork loin from a recently slaughtered hog in her Kelvinator, which she cut into chunks and dropped into the skillet. She added a tablespoon of rosemary, and then fetched a mason jar of rye whiskey from a hidden stash in the cellar. She poured in a quarter cup—it would add a husky undertone to the dish—and dropped in handfuls of rice.

The final touch would be fresh figs from Hog Island, Virginia. As she cut them open, exposing their white meat and dark red hearts, an aroma of flowers filled the

33

kitchen and Angela's childhood memories of summer life on that beautiful island came to her in a rush. Her family had a modest cottage at the edge of the little town of Broadwater, and a fig tree leaned compan-ionably against it, the wild descendant of a tree brought to the island hundreds of years ago. How she would dream of the place on long winter afternoons . . . the sand hills and pines, red cedar and honeysuckle, and the Island's flat beach, where the surf roared and one could run and run endlessly without a shadow in the vertical sunlight.

There was a bump at the screen door. It was the dogs. They looked in at Angela and turned to face three figures approaching through the loblolly pines by the creek.

The Revenuers that Bee had reported on the Leonard-town dock that morning were named Mullen and Mutter. They were retired police officers from south Philadelphia who left the city force with their pensions one week and started Federal employment with the Prohibition Unit the next. The double-dipping was good—they both supported large families that filled a pew at St. Paul's on Sunday—and Prohibition enforcement was a walk in the park compared with some nights in South Philly.

Mullen and Mutter were big men, and landlubbers to boot, so getting them safely into the Dart boat—a prize recently seized from a bootlegger—was a bit of a chore for the Coast Guard Lieutenant and Seaman who were assigned to them for the next several days.

"Lieutenant," said Mullen, "I don't know much about boats, but this looks like something that belongs on a lake."

"It *is* a lake boat, sir," said the Lieutenant with a smile as they motored away from the dock.

"Well, won't it get swamped or something if there are waves out there, God forbid?"

"We'll be alright, this boat can handle chop pretty well. We need the shallow draft boats to get into the creeks along the Potomac and the Bay."

Mullen engaged in his usual patter and within a half hour knew pretty much everything there was to know about the Lieutenant, his family, his hometown, his favorite sports teams, and his professional aspirations. "It's a nice age," thought Mullen to himself. "To be in your twenties, unmarried, in great physical shape, future wide open. I wouldn't live it again for a hundred trillion dollars, but it's nice while you're there."

The team spent the morning poking around a couple of farms on Newtown Neck and looked in at Flood Creek without result. By noon they were motoring into Poplar Hill Creek. The Lieutenant was steering them towards the eastern side of the creek, but Mullen pointed west and said, "Take us over to that side, there's something there."

They beached the boat and after a brief struggle with thorn bushes under the pines, they emerged on Angela's back lawn.

Mullen was leading the way but when Mutter saw the dogs on the porch he got out front and started a high whistle that was barely audible and seemed to confuse the dogs, who looked tentatively back into the house, where Angela had finished washing her hands. She came out to the porch.

She was the first really attractive woman Mullen had seen on this tour. Petite, dark eyes, long black hair, nice posture in a nice dress. Maybe twenty three or four. She looked ready for them—probably been called by a friend. Not everything was right in her world. He could tell that she'd been crying. Not today, probably last night. That look stayed around a woman's eyes long after it was over.

"We are federal Revenue agents, Miss," he said, holding up his shield, "and the Lieutenant is with the U.S. Coast Guard. We are responsible for enforcing the Volstead Act's prohibition against intoxicating liquors. We do not have a warrant to search this property, but we would like to talk to the owner."

"I'm the owner," said Angela, "but I'm busy cooking right now." She hesitated, but her good manners took over. "You're welcome to join me for lunch."

"That sounds wonderful. If you can put the dogs away first, we'd like that."

Angela seated the Revenuers and the Lieutenant at the breakfast table off the kitchen, and between carrying them plates of paella and pouring lemonade, answered a number of questions from Mullen, pushing back a little with each response. No, she had not seen unusual characters in the area, or unusual traffic on the roads or the water at night, and no, she did not know anyone engaged in moonshining or bootlegging, but even if she did, wasn't it his business to catch such people himself?

Mullen accepted these mild rebuffs in good humor and without surprise. In his personal opinion, Prohibition was the product of tiny bodies of crazed progressives with an unhealthy interest in ordering the lives of less evolved people through vast national programs—it was a mystery to him how they'd actually succeeded in getting the Constitution itself amended. But, by God this paella tasted good, especially the figs; if Mrs. Mullen knew how to cook like this, it would add another ten years to his life.

"Let me ask you," said Mullen, "do you grow rye in your fields?"

"Of course."

"Why, if not to make rye whiskey?"

At this point Angela sat down with a glass of lemonade, and looked Mullen in the eye. "You're not serious, are you?"

"I am. I don't know a thing about farming."

"These fields out here have probably been farmed in one way or another for the last thousand years. In fact, every time I have them plowed, Indian tools and arrowheads turn up. The soil here is a bit sandy, and with all the pressure over the years, it's short on nutrients. My fields are full of tobacco right now. It is an excellent cash crop, but the plants wear out the soil. So, I plant rye as a cover crop in winter. Rye has big roots that help aerate the soil and prevent erosion. When the rye is harvested in springtime, the roots and some clippings are plowed

under and deteriorate, making the ground ready for planting again. Here, let me fetch you another plate of paella."

Angela found the Coast Guard Lieutenant a pleasant-
looking fellow with a good smile. He was well-mannered,
sitting straight in his chair with his napkin on his lap and
his elbows off the table, giving her respectful but friendly glances. His attention, though, had wandered to the
shadow boxes hanging on the wall behind her.

"Say, Miss Doughty, may I ask what those medals are
for?"

She turned to look at them. "The one on the left is a
silver medal that was awarded to my father by the U.S.
Lifesaving Service."

"And the other medal, with the ribbon and the
certificate?"

"That is a medal of honor given to my father by the
government of Spain."

"That's extraordinary. What did he do?"

"He was part of the crew that rescued the survivors of
the *San Albano* off Hog Island."

❧   ❧   ❧

Winter, 1892
Hurricanes can be very terrible things in the tropics, a
grave threat to man and beast, but those that make it as
far north as the barrier islands of Virginia are usually old
storms, humid and uninspired, tossing the treetops about,
roughing up the ocean and dropping rain, here today and
gone tomorrow, spinning towards obscurity and death in
the north Atlantic.

If you prefer a new storm with snap and malice, one that will loiter for days, turning the ocean into a howling wasteland, throwing ice pellets and snow on the horizontal plane at fifty and sixty miles an hour, rearranging sandbars and islands with currents that surge like a river at the falls . . . well, that is the northeaster. It is born locally off the coast of the Carolinas, and may visit the Virginia shoreline between October and April—though most northeasters of any account seem to occur in February, when the conditions for creating human misery are at their sharpest edge.

Bill Doughty was living under the spell of one of these beauties in the darkness before dawn on February 23, 1892. He was Surfman #8 at the U.S. Life Saving Station on Hog Island. As the junior man on the Station, Bill was often assigned the midnight watch. In foul weather he took to the beaches looking for vessels in distress.

At 3:30 a.m., Bill was shuffling backwards into the wind, a walking stick in one gloved hand and a lantern in the other. Wet snowflakes the size of bumblebees were smacking into his head and shoulders. His oilskin jacket and leggings were dripping wet and clung to him like a shroud.

Every few minutes Bill would pause and look cautiously around the edge of his sou'wester out to sea—he did not want to catch a speeding snowflake in the eye. The dark over the ocean was absolute—the lowering grey clouds full of snow would have hidden a battleship. The big lantern in his left hand was no help. Hanging around knee height, the veteran of a thousand patrols, it had been so blasted by sand that its glass was frosted white and the light it gave off was little more than a friendly, homely kind of fog that reached just beyond Bill's feet. He took care not to look down at the lantern because it would ruin his vision and because the snow whipping through the little circle of light gave him a feeling of vertigo.

❦   ❦   ❦

It would be nice to say that Bill was an uncommonly brave and resolute young man, and that he walked the dunes with his chin forward, his keen grey eyes scanning the ocean for ships and steamers in peril, wearing that curious overlarge gunfighter's mustache that was common among surfmen. But that was not Bill. He was something of a romantic. The storm swells out beyond the breakers, great green domes that raised and lowered the horizon itself, were conforming to their own wild law that had nothing whatsoever to do with humankind, and they seemed to him a herd of wild beasts from a very old fable. When those swells felt the bottom and then pitched out and fell, trapping air and exploding on the shoals so that every grain of sand on the beach shivered and shook with the detonation, Bill felt awe and fear.

Bill was not an experienced waterman, and he was not an island man, though the little town of Broadwater on Hog Island was peppered with his kinfolk once and twice removed. Bill was an ocean swimmer. One summer day he'd dived off the railroad bridge at Lynnhaven Inlet and swam clear around Cape Henry down to Rudy Inlet. The walk home was harder than the swim. He did it again a couple of weeks later. And again the week following. It felt wonderful. In an era when people did not swim in the ocean for their health, it made Bill something of a curiosity and the *Norfolk Virginian* wrote a little article about him. His swim course took him past two life saving stations, which were unmanned in the summer months. However, William Payne, who was Keeper of the Seatack Life Saving Station, saw Bill churning by in the surf one afternoon as Payne was looking after some repairs to the station, and followed Bill until he came ashore.

"I've read about your exploits in the paper son," he told Bill. "Why do you do it?"

"I dunno sir. I guess I like it."

"Ever thought about joining the Life Saving Service?"

"No sir."

"Well, maybe you should. We don't do much swimming in the Service, point is to stay in the boat, not out, but your skill could come in handy. Do you drink?"

"No."

"Smoke?"

"No."

"Scare easy?"

"No."

"Live clean?"

Bill thought about that for a second—he wasn't sure what it meant, precisely—"I try, sir," he answered.

"Good. I know Johnny Johnson is looking for a junior surfman for his crew. You ever been to Hog Island?"

"No. Got relations there, I think."

"All the better. Prettiest island in the state. Johnson's a good man. I will write him a note mentioning your swimming skills if you care to give me your address."

And so Bill made his way into the Life Saving Service.

🟐   🟐   🟐

Being new to the Service, Bill had not participated in a serious rescue in a "whole storm," which was also known as a "Force 10" storm under the scale developed by Francis Beaufort of the Royal Navy for ships at sea. The definition of a whole storm was precise and bloodless: *"Very high waves with long over-hanging crests. The resulting foam, in great patches, is blown in dense white streaks along the direction of the wind. On the whole the surface of the sea takes on a white appearance. The 'tumbling' of the sea becomes heavy and shock-like. Visibility affected."*

The rational part of Bill's mind observed that only fools and madmen would go out in a Force 10 storm, but the dominant portion of his brain answered that a man curious to learn how bold he really was would undertake the risk, and perhaps even do it with a light heart. If a man entered that raging maelstrom and returned, what else was there to fear in life? The experience might create an overflowing well of confidence that a man could drink from again and again, for the rest of his days. For, what other earthly challenge would compare to climbing the near vertical walls of waves twenty feet high in a modest wooden boat? And what could be better than embracing such danger in the service of humanity? One had only to hear the joined voices of people in a shipwreck rising to a terrified chorus as a wave passed over them, or to see the pitiable remains of those lost in the struggle washing ashore, to know that the cause was a righteous one. The ocean should not be allowed to win. He, Bill Doughty, would not allow it.

Such were Bill's thoughts. They were not the thoughts of Keeper Johnny Johnson, or those of the veteran surf-men, who were technicians in the liquid element and for whom the saving of lives, ships and cargoes was all in a day's work, brutal though it may be. The weather, the sea state, the condition of the wrecked vessel and where she lay, along with the condition and capacity of her crew, were all parts of a puzzle. The puzzle needed to be solved with the tools available, whether that was the boat, breeches buoy, or the life car. The other ingredients for success—audacity, muscle, high-endurance and judgment on the part of the surfmen—were not regarded as tools at all, but as conditions precedent to life saving operations in winter on a wild coast. In other words, it was simply expected that the surfmen would be superior human beings.

Bill had a thick towel around his neck, but the unceasing wet snow had found the seams of his oilskin jacket and he felt the first finger of cold water moving down his left flank. The north wind was gusting now, letting up and then suddenly bearing down with a howl and yet more snow, seeking to push him off his feet. Bill was miles from the nearest warmth and shelter, utterly alone in the void of the storm, and growing wetter and colder by the minute. In his suffering Bill thought about the prophet Job of the Old Testament. There was a man who knew how to complain about wearisome nights and restlessness unto the dawning of the day. *"My days are swifter than a weaver's shuttle, and are spent without hope. O remember that my life is wind: mine eye shall no more see good!"* Yet, even in his whining poor old Job knew the Lord's eyes were upon him. Cheered by this thought Bill began to sing. "Michael, row the boat ashore, Hallelujah! Sister help him trim the sails, Hallelujah! Jordan's river is deep and wide, Hallelujah! And I've got a home on the other. . . ."

Unknown to Bill, over the course of the high tide in the night hours the ocean had attacked the dune line on Hog Island. Driving on shore at an angle and pushing the sea before it, the storm had set up a littoral current that swept down the beach at high speed and carried sand away by the hundreds of tons. This had sliced the primary dune in half, creating a vertical cliff eight feet high which ran for hundreds of yards along the oceanfront.

Singing and walking with his back to the wind, Bill stepped off this cliff and into space. He landed the full length of his body on the hard pan at the base of the cut, driving the air from his lungs. As he lay there struggling to breathe, a wall of water moving at high velocity across the narrow remains of the beach picked him up and flung him face first into the sand wall, and then pulled him back towards deeper water, filling his eyes, nose, ears and hair with suspended sand. The lantern was carried away by the retreating wave, but his walking stick was still attached to his wrist by a lanyard. Though disoriented and faint, Bill had the presence of mind to drive the stick into the sand and gain his feet. He began laboring back up the beach like an ice climber setting his pick on a mountainside, while the ocean surged around him.

For the next half hour, Bill stumbled along the sand wall, his left hand brushing its surface to balance and reassure him. When the remains of broken waves rose to the level above his waist, he planted the walking stick into the wall and held on with both hands until they subsided. He tried several times to climb up, but the wall was sheer, high and packed and gave him no purchase.

Bill's jacket contained a pouch of Coston signal flares, which surfmen carried to warn off vessels that were getting too close to shore. Bill lit one of these to find how narrow his world had become. In its red glare, he made out the shell-specked wall rising to his left, a band of wet sand no wider than a footpath at its base, and the storm surge to his right, racing at the wall, impacting it with a leap of spray and foam that went well overhead, and then pulling back in a rush. Bill told himself that the cliff had to end somewhere, and kept doggedly moving north.

The beach eventually began to widen and the height of the cut to diminish, until at last Bill was able to climb up to a stretch of firm ground. This ground was a mixture of peat and clay, what some call a "marsh mat." It was the shoreline of another age, when Hog Island was broad and heavily forested. The peat was usually covered by many feet of sand, but the current angling out of the northeast had laid it bare. Bill sat down to collect himself and empty his boots of water. He felt the snow slacking off and the wind moderating, but he had started to shiver and knew that it would grow worse if he did not get moving back to the station.

Bill's accident had made him cautious so he struck up a second flare to understand where he was. The peat was a black moonscape studded with the trunks of ancient trees and littered with white clam shells. It was an interesting sight and even in his anxiety to be gone Bill wandered about for a moment, gazing into the calm potholes of seawater dotting its surface. One held two seahorses that were dazed but upright and finning about. Another had a collection of barnacled whelk shells.

At the bottom of a deeper pool was a large gold coin, laying on a bed of sand and reflecting back the light of the flare. Bill lingered over it in surprise before pulling it out. The coin was a beautiful, heavy thing, featuring a portly king with laurels in his hair and the legend IOANNES.V.D.G.PORT.ET.ALG.REX around the rim. It was dated 1722. The reverse side featured a crown over a coat of arms.

Bill placed this carefully into his pocket and then fanned at the sand at the bottom of the pool. This uncovered a gold ring set with an emerald. He opened his jacket and put the ring inside his shirt pocket. Then the flare went out. That was alright—it was a feeling game now. Bill carefully sifted the sand through his fingers below the surface and recovered three more coins before he was satisfied the hole was empty.

Curious and wanting more, Bill crawled about until

he found another pool. He emptied it
of loose shells, and at the bottom felt
the firm, milled edge of another coin
between his chilled fingers. "Sweet Jesus,"
he murmured, "they're everywhere." He

hunted pothole after pothole by blind feel on his hands and
knees but was forced to stop when his shaking became so
violent that he had difficulty keeping hold of his finds. He
began walking south, his jacket pockets heavy with coins,
which gave off a satisfying clink with every step.

Gold has a powerful effect on the mind. Bill was wondering how much loot he'd left behind and how he could
quietly get back to the marsh mat at sunrise, when he happened to look out to sea. There, winking at him from the
direction of the outer shoals, was a white running light
on the fantail of a ship. Bill lit his remaining Coston flare
and waved it overhead until it burned out. When his eyes
readjusted to the darkness, he remained motionless for
long time, seeking the light, but it was gone. Making certain
that his pockets were fastened, Bill started jogging back in
the direction of the station. "Perhaps I just saved someone's
life," he thought, "they saw my flare and turned back out
to sea." And then he asked himself, "Wherever did this
treasure come from?"

❧   ❧   ❧

The crew of the steamship *San Albano*, out of the Spanish
port of Bilboa, had seen Bill's flare, and it gave them some
hope. On the evening of the 22nd, they had worked their
ship too far to the west in a vain search for the entrance

47

to Chesapeake Bay and wandered into the maze of submerged shoals that reached out from Hog Island. They were now trapped. Waves lifted the ship up and over one sandbar into a trough, where the crew placed two bow anchors, hoping to ride out the storm. But the giant swells proved too much, snapping the anchor lines and driving the ship backwards into another shoal, lifting her up and slamming her down on her keel with sickening violence. This lifting and dumping went on for several hours, moving the ship closer to the beach, but slowly opening her seams to the cold seawater. She finally ground out 500 yards from the island, laying broadside to the surf, which worked her over and began to break her up.

On his return to the station, Bill quietly put his treasures into several pairs of socks at the bottom of his footlocker. Then he shifted into dry clothes and slept on his cot for a couple of hours. At sunrise, he mentioned the white running light he had seen to Keeper Johnson, who climbed to the lookout atop the station and spotted the stack and masts of the *San Albano* far to the north.

🐟　　🐟　　🐟

So began the most grueling and legendary rescue ever conducted by the Life Saving Station on Hog Island. Johnson roused the entire crew. The eight of them, with a horse, pulled the thousand-pound beach apparatus containing their rescue gear five miles north into forty mile-an-hour winds over flooded country to the beach opposite the wreck. It took them two hours to get there.

They could see dozens of sailors waving madly from the deck houses atop the *San Albano*. Johnson had planned to use the breeches buoy to haul them off the wreck one by one, but the ship was too far out and the surf too high to risk it. He directed Bill and some other surfmen to fetch the surfboat and the life car, which were back at the station. Off they went, helped along by the wind. They hitched the station horse to the lifeboat, and a local team of horses to the life car, and went back up the beach. When they finally got there, it was two in the afternoon.

Bill had now walked 25 miles through this particular storm, some of it while soaked and chilled, and it was starting to show. He felt lightheaded and somewhat detached from it all, warm and strangely happy.

The surfmen set up their brass Lyle gun and fired a slug of lead with a small messenger line attached out to the *San Albano*. It was a perfect shot, but the ship's crew allowed the line to chafe against the rigging of the ship, and the line parted. A groan from the crew was carried to the surfmen on the wind.

The tide was rising, forcing the surfmen to retreat up the beach and increasing the distance to the wreck. They fired the Lyle gun again and again, increasing the black powder charge beyond safe levels, but after five attempts it was obvious it was not going to work.

"Ok, men," said Johnson, "we're going to try to reach the ship with the lifeboat! The current's running strong, so let's pull her up the beach a mile to try to drift down on the wreck. We need to hurry, we're losing daylight!"

The crew had practiced boat launches into the surf

a hundred times, but not in conditions like these. The waves striking the beach were standing six and eight feet high, sucking up pebbles and loose shells with a grinding clatter, and then hammering down, grey green and brown with sand. The surfmen watched the surf for a couple of minutes, trying to determine if there was a pattern here, but it was all a jumble, and when Johnson yelled, "Let's go!" they tightened their grips on the gunnels and ran into it, flipping into the boat and digging deep with their oars, which hardly seemed to get a bite in the air-charged water.

Bill was at the front of the life boat, pulling his oar in cadence with the others. Several waves were so steep that he could look down at Johnson at the tiller and feel himself lightening on the bench, where another degree to the vertical would have pitched them all into the boils of white water. "Row, men, row!" shouted Johnson, "we need to get out!" The surfboat crawled east towards the wreck but the current was running south with the speed of a millrace and they swept past the *San Albano* with hundreds of yards to go. "Okay, boys, half speed, we're not going to get there," said Johnson.

Bill turned to have a look at the ship but could see nothing but smoking waves. The sky was thinning to the west. There wasn't much there, a washed out red and yellow with no warmth.

Somehow the crew made it back to shore, the boat half awash. Johnson had a look at the men. They were still fresh enough. Doughty was sucking wind and his color was up, but Johnson credited that to excitement. "Let's get the boat on the cart and pull it two miles above the wreck, we're going to have another try."

The second rescue attempt brought them far closer to the *San Albano*, so close that the Spanish crew were throwing weighted lines towards the surfboat in an effort to snag her. Johnson urged the surfmen on at the top of his lungs, trying to angle the boat into the lee of the ship. The current was profound—Johnson had never seen anything like it—moving so fast that the *San Albano*, grounded as she was, appeared to be under power with a wake streaming behind her. Nothing could live in it. The men were giving it everything they had, pulling well in time, but they were losing ground, and the gap between the ship and the lifeboat began to grow. It was then that a human form detached itself from the deck of the ship and dropped into the sea.

Bill heard a roar of voices from the *San Albano* and whipped his head round to see the Spaniards lining the rail of the ship and a single, pale arm rising from the water. He had his boots off in a moment and heard Johnson's "No!" as he cleared the gunwale and struck out in the direction of the other swimmer. The freezing water felt great—he had been burning up in the lifeboat. Bill was wearing a cork life-jacket but it hardly seemed to slow him as he paddled wildly towards the little figure out in front of him, a figure rising and falling with each wave but seeming to struggle less and less with every passing second.

It was just him and that other person now. The ship was fading from view, and the surfboat was gone, and the light was going, the ocean turning a flat purple and blue. Bill reached the figure, threw his arm across its chest, and began stroking back towards the beach, which was unreeling before his eyes like a picture show. "It's alright," he told himself, "I can do this forever." He held on to his burden through the plunging and backing waves over a series of sandbars and then through the shore pound, where he finally gained his feet. He hefted the victim over his shoulder and walked up the steep, packed beach. The victim had a lot of long, black hair that was blowing back and clinging to his face. He thought it was nice—it smelled like cocoanuts. He saw people running towards them and laid the victim down on the sand. "How strange," he thought, "it's a lady," and then he passed out.

❧   ❧   ❧

Bill's raging fever carried him along over the next two days on a current of its own. He would sleep and see the black mote of his rescue rising on a wave in front of him and he would swim with everything he had and it would keep moving away from him. He would see a beautiful girl with ebony hair down in the deep and go after her, his lungs bursting. And then he would be on fire and sweating and struggling to climb back to the surface, the girl urging him on, her hands on his face.

He awoke one evening, very late. The girl from his dreams was sitting next to his cot in Keeper Johnson's stuffed leather chair. She looked small in it. A beach lantern was burning low on the table beside her. She was fast asleep, her arms crossed and her head down, a book on her lap. Bill looked at her for a long time, and then dozed off.

She was there in the morning, offering him chicken broth in a bowl. She spoke to him in broken English. Her name was Roxalana. Her uncle, Jose A. De Sagarraga, was the captain of the *San Albano*. She cooked on board the ship. She had wanted to see the world. Now, she was not so sure, she said, laughing. She pulled her hair behind one ear, smiling easily with even, white teeth. Bill was spellbound.

"You save me," she said, pointing between them. "You my hero, yes?"

Bill gave a wan smile in return.

She held his hand, and leaned forward, looking directly into his eyes. "You my hero. That everything." She kissed his burning forehead. "I come back. How you say, lunch, then come back."

Bill's next visitor was Keeper Johnson. He settled into his easy chair next to Bill's cot with a sigh.

"Bill, you'll be glad to know that the crew of that steamship are alive and well. A few of them made it off the wreck in a boat, and the rest we took off in the life car the day after you rescued Miss Roxalana."

"I'm glad, Captain," said Bill, "I didn't think we could do it."

"The bad news is that you've been laid up for four days. You've got pneumonia in your lungs and you're not really improving. You're too sick for us to treat here. I am going to ship you up to the Marine Hospital in Cambridge, where they can take better care of you. Do you understand?"

Bill nodded.

"We've got a bit of a problem with senorita Roxalana. She insists that she is going to stay with you at the hospital until you're recovered. She won't budge. Captain De Sagarraga is raising holy hell. Do you have some kind of understanding with her?"

"I'm very fond of her," said Bill in a weak breath.

"I'm afraid that "fond" is not going to cut it with the Captain. She's not only his cook, she's his blood relation! These people are Catholics from old Castile, Bill, you don't wander off with one of their women folk just because you're fond of her. I don't want this station getting some kind odd reputation in the Service or having the Captain and the Spanish consulate saying bad things about us."

"I'm sorry," croaked Bill.

"It's not entirely your fault." Johnson paused. "Let me ask you plain, Bill: do you like her enough to marry her?"

Bill had never seriously courted a girl. But he recalled something his father once told him, which was, "Bill, if you're sick and passed out on the floor and she's still taking care of you, stop looking because you've got a winner."

"I think so," he told Johnson.

"Good. Do you think she'd marry you?"

"I don't know. I guess I'd need to ask her."

Johnson brightened up. "Well, it's a start. If she says yes, I can get the Reverend Sturgis in here to perform a wedding service. The Captain can hardly complain when she's a married woman!"

When Johnson left, Bill rose weakly from bed and opened his footlocker. He untied one of his socks and pulled the emerald ring out. Then he climbed back into bed, shaking with cold. He looked at the ring. It was as ponderous as he remembered, a rich yellow gold with a square-cut emerald that was a clear, deep green. "Well," he thought, "if she says no it won't be on account of the ring."

┾┾ ┾┾ ┾┾

Summer, 1923

As Angela was cleaning up after lunch, the Revenuers and the Coast Guard Lieutenant walked around to the front of the house. There was a hog pen off the dirt drive that bordered the woods. There were three hogs in it. Two were fast asleep, while a third was busy licking the remains of its meal from a wooden trough with gusto and grunts. Seeing them, it made as though to come over and say hello, but after taking several erratic steps, the hog stopped, gave a loud belch and flopped on its side.

"Look at those things!" said Mullen. "I'm no farmer, but I can tell when a hog is *stonato*. I can smell it, too. They've been eating rye mash from a still." He looked across the tobacco fields towards the distant tree line. There was a big, single oak tree towering above the pines. "She'll have her still somewhere by that oak. I'd guess it's not a small one, either. It won't be industrial, but it will be big."

But then Mullen noticed something else, two little rounded white nicks at the edge of the shade thrown by the oak tree.

"Lieutenant, you've got younger eyes than I do, what are those white things?"

"They're tombstones, sir. They look new." The Lieutenant

rubbed his chin. "Uh, I think that I read about this in one of our weekly reports. Yeah, I've got it. It was in March or April. A male and female in their forties or fifties were pulled out of the water about a mile off Point Lookout. Their capsized boat was found miles away on the main stem of the Bay. They must have swum for shore, but you can't survive long in water that cold. I heard later that the male was a retired surfman. It must have been Doughty and his wife. He did pretty good under the circumstances, was probably towing her along. But you can't swim forever, you just can't."

Mutter crossed himself, gave a negative shake of the head to Mullen, and began walking back to the boat.

"What are you going to do?" the Lieutenant asked Mullen.

"Well, Lieutenant, I think it's up to you to tell her over dinner in Leonardtown this weekend that she'd better lay off making whiskey or she's going to get into real trouble."

"Over dinner?" said the Lieutenant, with genuine surprise.

"Well sure," said Mullen. "She comes from good people, you come from good people, why don't you ask her out? Take your time, I'll be down at the boat with the others." As he walked away, Mullen threw over his shoulder, "When you see a jewel, son, you need the wisdom to pick it up."

4

Blackbeard's Burgoo

Burgoo *is an interesting word and an even more inter-*esting food. As a word, we can trace its origins to the foredeck of eighteenth-century sailing ships, where all speech was rounded off around a plug of tobacco. As a food, burgoo defies a ready definition. To the sailor, it could mean a gruel of dense grey oatmeal, or it might mean something far more splendid. Perhaps something as splendid as the last meal enjoyed by Captain Edward Teach, the pirate better known to us as Blackbeard.

⚜   ⚜   ⚜

[I]n Blackbeard's Journal, which was taken,
there were several Memorandums of the fol-
lowing Nature, sound writ with his own
Hand.—Such a Day, Rum all out:—Our
Company somewhat sober:—A damn'd Confu-
sion amongst us!—Rogues a plotting;—great
Talk of Separation.—So I look'd sharp for a
Prize;—such a Day took one, with a great deal

57

of Liquor on Board, so kept the Company hot,
damned hot, then all Things went well again.

FROM *A GENERAL HISTORY OF THE PYRATES,*
BY CAPTAIN CHARLES JOHNSON, LONDON,
PRINTED FOR, AND SOLD BY T. WARNER, AT
THE BLACK-BOY IN PATER-NOSTER-ROW, 1724.

Blackbeard is the pirate name above all other names in the Tidewater region. Every local map remembers him. There is a Blackbeard's Hill, Blackbeard's Point, and Blackbeard's Island in the lower Chesapeake Bay; a Blackbeard's Bluff in the upper Bay; and heaven alone knows how many Blackbeard's Coves in between.

In this era of innumerable moving pictures about swashbuckling pirates, it is difficult not to feel something of a smile coming on as Messrs. Errol Flynn, Burt Lancaster, or Yul Brenner cheerfully swing from the mainmast with spyglasses and open shirts. Tales of brigands and daring deeds have ever been popular, but it is right to be concerned that writers and film-makers may so reduce the story of piracy to lampoon or camp that a future generation might be more inclined to laugh at the figure of a pirate, rather than to take wonder at the rise of such wild men on the very doorstep of young America.

The truth is as strange and colorful as any fiction. Colonists along the eastern seaboard took alarm at the nick of a strange sail appearing suddenly at dusk off the coastal approaches to their little towns. Their vessels were boarded and sunk, their towns raided, their homes pilfered, their slaves carried away, and their people held hostage. Pitched sea battles under the black flag took

58

place in our neighborhood, featuring challenges and curses, broadsides, boarders, cutlass fights, flintlock pistols fired into the body at point blank, with red blood pouring from the scuppers.

Captain Teach's story started in the Caribbean, where he served in the Royal Navy during the Queen Anne's War, a long and unremembered scuffle that ranged from Europe to the Americas and the Caribbean. At war's end, unemployed sailors like Teach sometimes turned pirate to sustain themselves.

Blackbeard made common cause with other notorious pirates headquartered in the town of New Providence, Bahamas, what we now call Nassau. It was a perfect base of operations. It was lawless and from its harbors and inlets pirates could strike at a constellation of good targets, including the Spanish Main and the Mid-Atlantic colonies from the Carolinas to Delaware.

Captain Teach was a "black meteor" that crossed that constellation with wild success, capturing prize upon prize from 1716 to 1718, appearing to be everywhere at

once: shaking down a crew off Bermuda; lurking off the mouth of the Chesapeake; blockading Charleston harbor; burning ships in Honduras; careening in Grand Cayman; robbing sloops in the Delaware; and capturing a French

guineaman loaded with jewels, gold dust and plate off St. Vincent.

Blackbeard was famous in his own day. He was a tall

and powerful man, with a commanding presence. To dishearten merchant crews during a capture, he placed slow-burning fuses into his hair and beard, and boarded them wreathed in smoke. Where pirates were notorious for the abuse and murder of captives, Blackbeard employed intimidation alone—it seldom failed him.

It is said that Captain Teach married some thirteen trollops and doxies during his adventures in various ports. But he fell truly in love with the young daughter of a planter in Bath Town, a quiet spot off Pamlico Sound in North Carolina. Because the Crown was then offering a "pardon" to pirates he surrendered to the colony's governor, Charles Eden, who later officiated at his wedding. Teach built a home for his wife in Bath, but spent little time in it. He was only a few hours sail from Ocracoke Island, where he anchored behind the outer banks and looked for passing prizes, when he was not cruising the Main.

❦   ❦   ❦

P.S. Here is advice of a considerable event in these parts, that the Spanish Plate Fleet richly laden, consisting of eleven sail, are, except one, lately cast away in the Gulf of Florida to the southward of St. Augustin, and that a barcolongo sent from the Havanna to fetch off from the Continent some passengers of distinction, who were in that Fleet, having recovered from the wrecks a considble. quantity of plate is likewise cast away about 40 miles to the

*northwd. of St. Augustin. I think it my duty to
inform H.M. of this accident, which may be
improved to the advantage of H.M. subjects if
encouragement be given to attempt the recov-
ery of that immense treasure.*

LETTER OF ALEXANDER SPOTSWOOD, LIEUTENANT-
GOVERNOR OF THE COLONY OF VIRGINIA, TO THE
COUNCIL OF TRADE, OCTOBER 24, 1715

The Governor of the Crown Colony of Virginia,
Alexander Spotswood, in the tradition of many a colonial governor before him, came to America to make his
fortune. Like Blackbeard, he was a veteran of the Queen
Anne's War, and a man of action.

Between thrashing the hapless locals in the House of
Burgesses, Spotswood paid great attention to keeping as
much peace as could be had with the Indians, at which
he was quite skilful and equitable. He gobbled up large
portions of land, and led a large drinking and shooting
party into the wilderness for several weeks, known ever
after as "The Knights of the Golden Horseshoe." He had
four children. Spotswood's descendants were to include a
son who died while serving under George Washington; a
grandson who married Washington's niece; and a grand-
daughter who married Patrick Henry.

Knowing that the Spanish had lost untold millions on
the shallow Florida reefs in 1715 when its entire treasure
fleet was surprised by a hurricane, Spotswood outfitted
an expedition of Virginians to "lend assistance" to the
Spanish in their salvage efforts. The expedition team
was promptly captured by the Spaniards on its arrival in

Florida, and confined to the gloomy dungeons of Morro Castle in Havana. Only one man returned alive.

The pirates out of Nassau were equally fascinated by the sinking of the plate fleet. When the Spanish and their Indian divers had stacked pyramids of 70-pound bar silver on the beach, alongside chests of gold doubloons and great bags of silver coins, pirate raiding parties swooped in, drove the salvage crews into the mangroves, scooped up the treasure and returned to Nassau for celebration. The unfortunate Spaniards had frequent visits from the 'Brethren of the Coast' wanting a fresh supply of the finest money that was ever minted.

Governor Spotswood, hearing rumors of Blackbeard's great successes in the Caribbean, annoyed by his predation on local shipping, and rightly suspecting that the government of impoverished North Carolina was colluding with pirates, outfitted an armed party to check in at the pirate's favorite haunt on Ocracoke.

Spotswood leased two sloops at his own expense—it would be thus easier for him to claim any treasure found on Blackbeard's ship or at his home in Bath—and manned them with sailors from the *Pearl* and *Lyme*, two English men-of-war then anchored in the James River. The sloops were placed under the command of Lieutenant Robert Maynard of the *Pearl*. A separate overland party led by the captain of the *Lyme* was to descend on Bath by horse. On November 17, 1718, the expedition left Virginia for the Carolina coast.

🦜　　🦜　　🦜

Maynard boarded him, and to it
They fell with sword and pistol too;
They had Courage, and did show it,
Killing of the Pirate's Crew.
Teach and Maynard on the Quarter,
Fought it out most manfully,
Maynard's Sword did cut him shorter,
Losing his head, he there did die.

FROM *THE DOWNFALL OF PIRACY,* ATTRIBUTED TO
YOUNG BENJAMIN FRANKLIN

Blackbeard's last stand off Ocracoke Island in his
sloop *Adventure* is the stuff of legend, and well docu-
mented. Lieutenant Maynard's sloops pulled up outside
Ocracoke inlet at sundown on Thursday, November 21.
They attacked the following day, and a wild sea fight
ensued between the pirates and navy men, with Blackbeard felled from behind the moment he was about to
finish Maynard with a sweep of his cutlass.

The pirate had five pistol shots in him and twenty
severe cuts at the time of his death. After clapping the
surviving pirates in irons, Maynard's men chopped off
Blackbeard's head, hung it from the bowsprit of their
sloop, and sailed to Bath Town for the planned treasure
hunt. Though they searched his house, local barns and
haystacks, they found no treasure.

Blackbeard's skull was later stuck on a pike and dis-
played at the entrance to Hampton Roads as a warning
to other pirates. Still later, someone pulled it down and
had silver laid over it. It then served as a punch bowl at

the Raleigh Tavern in Williamsburg.

It is said that records of the admiralty proceedings against Blackbeard's crew, held in the General Court-room of the Capital of Williamsburg on March 12, 1719, were destroyed by fire or lost.

But they were not lost; the records were carried away by unknown hands and have been held for generations in the same clasped Spanish ironwood box where the crown of Blackbeard's great skull, lined with silver, is kept safe. Few living people have seen "Blackbeard's Cup." The Honorable Charles Harry Whedbee thought he drank corn whiskey from it in a secret ceremony on Ocracoke in the 1930s, but he was not sure.

Those who care for the pirate's relics assure us that when the cup is removed from its hiding place, and only during a full moon in November, it is filled to the brim with the finest untaxed low country liquor, and drained by those assembled swearing "Death to Spotswood!"

And so on to our recipe, which is contained in the fragile, yellowed papers from the trial of Blackbeard's crew, which are now some 243 years old.

The inquisitor in the excerpt below is unknown. He does not appear highly skilled at examining witnesses, as his questioning of Captain William Bell shows. Yet it may also be true that Captain Bell (who was not charged as a pirate), was not inclined to be helpful. He was not a Virginian, but a native of Currituck. His loyalty may have resided with his own province of North Carolina, which regarded Governor Spotswood's expedition as a wrongful "invasion" of its poorer southern neighbor.

The examinations is as follows:

"What is your name?"

"It is Bell, William Bell, Captain."

"How came you to be in Cherock on the 22nd of November of last year?"

"The rudder of my snow, the *Nancy*, was carried off when we strucke a shoal off Whalebone Inlet during the afternoon watch of the 21st. The current carried us north and I aimed by shifting sail to put into Portsmouth, but the flood was too stronge so I contrived to put in behind the hook at Cherock and run her to the beach."

"What happened then?"

"I lit my pipe."

"And what happened after that?"

"I took a nap."

"Nay, what ye Commissioners wish to know is what you saw."

"I watched the sun then sette."

"Did you encounter any other living persons at Cherock?"

"Aye. A boat put off from shoare where there was a great bonfire. The man in the boat said his captain invited us to sup, and me, the mate, two hands and the boy went to shoare with him."

"And what did you see there?"

"Being hungry, my eye was attracted to the

great iron cauldron a bubblin' over the fire."

"What...."

"And there were great loaves of new made bread, too. They also caught my eye."

"Now, Captain Bell, I feel that it is necessary to warn you that you are under oath, and have been brought here so that this Court may determine the guilt or innocence of the men here charged with piracy. Please confine your testimony to relevant facts."

"But I don't know what you mean by relevant or by facts. Me memory works like this: I see one thing in my mind. Then I see the next. And after that I see the next. I don't jump one over the other because something important might be missed in the jumping, you see?"

"Well, then, I suppose we will get there in time. Please continue."

"The mate and I drew closer to the pot, which gave off a most pleasing smell. There were rough fellows all around. We shared their rum. A great tall feller, Tache, was their captain and him I had heard of. He was friendly like, and we came to talking about the victuals in the pot. Said he, 'It ain't a stew! It's burgoo, mate. Ye start her slow in the morning over low coals, just water and hard corn. Pluck a soft pullet or two, throw 'em in. Use jungle fowl if you ain't got chiken, but never turkey. Always add a splash of rum from your bottle. Go slow, mate, let her simmer. Add hog or mutton and their bones to your liking. If they're in short supply, possum, coon or squirrel will do. Add more rum! Find yourself some taters or beans—in they go! Cook low for a watch or two. Give it a stir now and again. Finish with Mexican chili and more rum—we have plenty of both, don't we lads,' says he with a laugh."

"Thank you for that narrative, Captain Bell, but. . . ."

"But there is the next thing, sir. Seeing our hunger he took a great ladle from the fire and shared a dish of burgoo, into which I dipped the bread. He watched me very closely as I took my first bite. I pronounced it most savory and satisfying, and he smiled with a great grin, all great white teeth, and shook my hand. I seen that his eyes, though red from drinking, were a dark blue. He gazed past me then, out across the sandbar to the ocean side, where we could see against the stars the bare poles of two vessels, newly come to anchor."

"What then happened?"

"Well. His troubles began soon after that."

5

Surf 'n Sky Crab Cakes

The Meridian Club is a venerable place that sits inside Bennett Point on the Wye River. The Club does three things for its members: provides perfect natural amphitheatres for Sporting Clays on two of the dozen coves bounded by the property; offers 27 holes of golf where most shots to the green are over water; and makes the finest crab cakes in the state of Maryland in its little kitchen.

No one seems to know how to become a member of the Meridian. It appears to be an ancestral and marital privilege, with an occasional invitation quietly extended to a couple or family who seem to have the right attributes—yet no one knows what those attributes are. There are members who have great wealth and those who have old names, and some who have neither.

The Meridian hosts no wedding ceremonies and no receptions. There are no planned holiday parties and no Sunday brunches. Doubtless there is a governing board of some kind, but the names of its officers will not be found on any plaque. There are no photographs of members past or present hanging on the walls. The Club does not refer back to itself or celebrate its own existence. It is simply there, down a long, shaded, oyster shell lane, a pink-brick Georgian structure in Flemish header bond, rising from a jumble of climbing rose bushes.

The main hallway of the clubhouse opens to the great "new" room, which has a large stone fireplace on the west end, a panoramic view of Shaw Bay through soaring windows, and a second fireplace on the east end, with deep leather sofas, chairs, and low tables between them. To the rear, there is a distinctive bar of American chestnut and checkered osage, which is properly loaded with top-shelf brands. The bar connects to the kitchen through a swinging door.

The new room has paintings which at first glance look like a higher grade of the usual rod and gun stuff, but several are signed by Winslow Homer. For unknown reasons—perhaps it was a gift that could not be refused—there is a Maxfield Parrish hanging in a discreet corner, where a lightly dressed nymph looks thoughtfully across an impossible landscape with her chin upon her knee. There are also decoys on shelves, a canvasback pair carved by Daddy and James Holly, several drakes and hens from the Dye brothers, and a small flotilla of Red Breasted Mergaser shaped by the Wards.

＊ ＊ ＊

It is lunchtime on a Saturday in the middle of March. The trees are stark and the Wye is glittering cold, but as often happens at this time of year, a spell of warm air and sunshine has come up from the south, and the club is busy with golfers.

Three women are ensconced in a corner couch. They have played nine holes of golf and will play nine more, but not before having a crab cake sandwich. The two older ladies are life-long members, and very much at home as they wave lazily to Paul behind the bar. They winter on Jupiter Island, where they are neighbors, and are deeply tanned, with arms toned by striking thousands of golf balls since the Thanksgiving holidays. Each lights up a Lucky Strike and sinks into the cushions of the couch with sighs of satisfaction—both are below par on the front nine.

The third woman is a guest, much younger than her companions, and has no tan at all. Everything is new to her—she's not been to the Meridian before, though she's of course heard about it for years. She was concerned that it might be a snooty high-ho kind of place, and is relieved that it is not. She likes it that no one in this cheerful room seems too preoccupied with looking at one another, or at her. She is also happy that no one has expressed surprise that she's already lost eight balls in the water.

"Good afternoon, ladies," says Paul, "Mrs. Phipps, Mrs. Bernard." He gives the young lady a nod.

"Hello Paul," says Mrs. Phipps. "We'd like three crab cake sandwiches, please. Betty and I will each have a Sidecar."

To their young companion she says, "How about you, Kathy, something fruity? Yes? No alcohol in that one, Paul."

Paul brings the drinks and sandwiches and then disappears into the kitchen. After an experimental sip of her cocktail, Mrs. Phipps asks, "Kathy, can you be a dear and have Paul put a little more bourbon in here?"

At the bar, Kathy notices a medallion fixed to the door that enters the kitchen. It is round, and brass, about eight inches across. It features a bas relief portrait of a man with a strong jaw, a straight nose, and rather long hair with a flip at the end. Below the portrait in bold, neoclassical letters, are the words "Red Carroll."

It seems that everyone in the new room is eating a crab cake sandwich, from an octogenarian couple in canvas DuxBak shooting vests down to some young boys in golf togs who are covertly admiring (again) the female figure in the Parrish painting. The crab cakes are handsome, perfectly shaped like oversized hockey pucks, a toasted, mottled brown steaming between fresh made buns.

On returning with Mrs. Phipps' perfected Sidecar, Kathy takes a bite of her crab cake sandwich. It's not her natural choice for food, but Mrs. Phipps seemed rather enthused about them on the drive over, and Kathy does not want to give offense. Kathy's had her share of crab cakes before—the insipid, crumbly kind that cannot hold itself together; the dense kind made primarily of bread crumbs that requires two tall beverages to consume; and the deep fried kind that tastes like the crabs lived out their lives in an engine room. This crab cake, however, is of a different kind. It is light but has a pleasant substance to it—she feels as though she's having an actual meal as she bites into its crunchy surface—and it has a tart, creamy aftertaste that is very pleasant.

"My, this sandwich is delightful," says Kathy, receiving smiles in return. "Tell me, who is the man on the kitchen door?"

"Oh, the medallion," says Mrs. Phipps. "That was put up years ago to honor Red Carroll. He was the cook here for a time, in the early thirties I think. God bless him."

"God bless him indeed," adds Mrs. Bernard. "But Betty, he was not really a cook. He was more like a chef de cuisine."

"Well, I don't recall that he'd graduated from any culinary school."

"True. But he was not a cook. A cook is someone who drops things into a fryer."

"I see your point. He was something more. A self-taught artist. Perhaps a *gastronome*."

"Yes, a gastronome in the best sense of the word. He was all of that. God bless him."

Mrs. Phipps nods. "Red Carroll brought goodness with him. God bless him, wherever he might be."

᷂   ᷂   ᷂

Long before these blessings descended on his head, Red Carroll had attended the Baltimore Polytechnic Institute on North Avenue and Calvert Street in Baltimore. The white halls of that elite high school seemed to have an Olympian glow about them, and Red plunged into the standard curriculum favoring math and elementary science with zeal. He took naturally to practical instruction in mechanical drawing, carpentry, sheet metal, and electricity, and graded well. Red assumed, with the encouragement of his parents, that he would go on to a career in mechanical engineering.

BPI's football coaches, always mindful of the annual Thanksgiving Day contest against Baltimore City College, took quick notice of Red. He was hard to ignore, as he stood a head taller than his classmates, and that head was covered with unusual volumes of copper hair. His movements were fluid and he had obvious speed. "Can you throw?" they asked him, "We'll train you as a quarterback. If you want to catch, we'll make you a tight end." He politely declined their numerous offers.

The coaches eventually appealed to Principal Wilmer Dehuff for assistance, but following a brief interview with Red in his office, Dr. Dehuff said, "The kid doesn't want play, leave him alone." At Poly-City games, which BPI seemed to lose with annoying frequency, the coaches shot dark looks at Red, who loitered in the stands with his friends, almost unconscious of the pretty girls who seemed to surround him like filings attracted to a magnet.

Though Red suffered little of the spotted, mopish lassitude common to teenage boys, he could still have his head turned by glittering but less useful academic topics, such as Ancient History and Latin.

It was at Christmas dinner in 1930, after his father had treated the family to a long, familiar monologue on how the Hoover Administration was destroying trade in Baltimore with tariffs on foreign goods, that Red stood and proclaimed to his wondering parents and siblings:

"*When the occasion demands it, Father, you can expand and amplify with strength and majesty; and you know when to be concise with energy! Your periods flow with ease, and your composition has every grace of style and sentiment! You command the passions with resistless sway . . . posterity will do you ample justice!"*

"That was very nicely done, Randall," said his mother. "What was it?"

"Why, that was from Tacitus' Dialogue Concerning Oratory, Mother. I memorized it for Latin class. I do so enjoy oratory that I might take to the stage. Planning for college is all very fine, but a man needs a break from his studies, to live a little."

His parents looked at one another. "Randall," said his father, "where did you pick up that piece of philosophy?"

"I believe I read it in *The Adventures of Jimmie Dale*."

"But Jimmy Dale is a fictitious character, Randall. And if I recall correctly, Jimmy Dale had a Harvard degree and inherited a fortune, so he was free to do as he liked."

"That's true."

"And I think that you've mixed up oratory and acting. The two are not the same."

This initial conversation progressed into the common arguments that fathers and sons have at this stage of life, and ended as usual in something of a compromise: the country was experiencing a great depression of the economy; new jobs for engineers might be scarce for years; and jobs for new actors might not be so scarce. Randall could have a single year to follow the stage before moving on to college; he would learn, perhaps the hard way, what it meant to earn a living among the working classes; and he was on no account to pursue a relationship with anyone identifying herself as an actress.

The day after graduating with BPI's class of 1931, Red started looking for his acting job.

◄   ◄   ◄

Locals and summer residents along the shores of the West River were living in a state of suspense going into the third week of July in 1931. Even wizened old crabbers coming and going from the county wharf in Galesville would sometimes lift their heads and gaze off to the northeast, listening carefully for a moment before resuming work. Children started to show up on the wharf and on neighborhood docks shortly after sunup, skipping barefoot down Main Street, dangling their legs over the water, asking lots of questions and generally getting in the way. An unusual noise across the water would bring them to a full stop, their heads swiveling as one, all gazing up towards Cedar Point and the open Chesapeake Bay.

It was the posters that got the whole thing started. A couple of evenings back, a tan Buick McLaughlin rolled quietly into the neighborhood. There was a man behind the wheel and there was another man standing on the running board with a leather apron full of brass tacks and a little hammer. His name was W.H. Aldredge and he was what they call an Advance Man. Every hundred yards or so, Aldredge would hop off with a poster and tap it into place on whatever vertical surface he could find. When he was done, there were blazing red, orange and yellow bills posted all over the surrounding countryside.

This is what the posters said:

COMING! COMING! COMING!
THE ORIGINAL FLOATING THEATRE!
VAUDEVILLE—GIRLS—DRAMA—
MIRTH—ROMANCE!

It was on a Sunday morning just before noon when it happened. A dozen families were having ham and eggs at the restaurant on Zang's Pier, some still dressed for church. The faithful would have to agree that the Good Lord made each of us one soul and body at a time, and made us rational creatures with five obvious senses, but in His wisdom He also made us creatures that sometimes share a common consciousness, a kind of telepathy. At the height of the meal, when everyone was talking, dishes were clattering, the salt was being passed and the coffee filled, there came a sudden pause and no one talked and nothing moved. Then a young boy in a crooked bow tie burst through the restaurant door and shouted, "The Show Boat's here!" His little sister, close on his heels in her Sunday dress, stopped, filled her lungs and screamed.

The Show Boat was here. As its front edge glided silently around Cedar Point, magnified in the undulating summer atmosphere, it looked impossible, a gigantic rectangular wedding cake suspended in air. On and on she came, 122 feet long and two storeys high, dwarfing the pleasure craft that darted around her like excited water bugs. The crowds filling the wharves at Galesville could see the two tugs flanking her, the *Trouper* and the *Elk*, maneuvering her majestic bulk in the channel, and propelling her forward at a surprising pace.

The Show Boat loomed ever closer, white and gigantic, colorful pennants and flags snapping in the breeze. She seemed too big, too glamorous to possibly fit against the little wooden toothpick of the county wharf. But the veteran tug crews had many seasons and thousands of landings behind them, up the skinny water of rivers, creeks and coves to hamlets, villages and towns from North Carolina to Delaware. They neatly slowed her and turned her broadside to the excited crowd on the wharf, where everyone could read JAMES ADAMS FLOATING THEATRE in large block letters on her upper works.

The entire cast of the Theatre lined the rails dressed in their most ornate costumes. As one, they began to sing Kern and Hammerstein's *Make Believe*:

"Only make believe I love you, Only make believe that you love me, Others find peace of mind in pretending, Couldn't you? Couldn't I? Couldn't we?"

Red Carroll was in costume as a Country Swain, a close-fitting chamois affair with a rakish hat and long yellow feather. The costume was scratchy and hot. Like other young male troupers on the Show Boat, he was obliged to perform several nautical duties. This included manning the fenders and mooring ropes on arrival in port. Red sang the closing lines of *Make Believe* with gusto as he gathered up a 3-inch line and jumped to the wharf to tie her off.

"Hey there, are you one of the actors?" asked a bedazzled lass.

"I'm not an actor, miss," said Red with a smile, "I'm a thespian."

"You're a what?"

Red's answer was drowned by the steam whistle of the tug *Elk*, which then began loading the Show Boat's 10-piece band to take the word to the countryside. The *Elk* would nose into Hopkins Cove over in Shady Side and look into Popham Creek before cruising down to Deale and Chesapeake Beach, noisily sounding her whistle as she went, the band crashing away to good effect with cymbals, drums and horns.

The Show Boat was in town, and everyone ought to know.

><del>◄</del>   ><del>◄</del>   ><del>◄</del>

When Red Carroll joined the company of the James Adams Floating Theatre, it was just coming off the pinnacle of indirect fame. Without national attention, the Theatre had faithfully carried its plays, vaudeville acts and music to some 94 ports of call throughout the Tidewater Region for almost two decades, operating 37 weeks out of the year with a different production six nights of the week—a punishing pace for a company of ten actors. The company might be small, but its audiences were not—the Theatre (which was constructed atop a converted lumber barge) could seat 850 people.

There were clerics who objected to the Floating Theatre's plays on moral grounds—of themselves, the racy titles of home-grown productions like 'She Knew What She Wanted' and 'Cheating Woman' raised eyebrows—but the isolated peoples of the Tidewater, white and black, young and old, simply loved the Theatre, delighted with her tales of heroes and villains, romances and family dramas, all of which ended with a decent moral point and usually with happiness for those who deserved it.

It was the interesting novelist Edna Ferber who immortalized the James Adams Floating Theatre—sort of. In April of 1925, she left New York and beat the bushes down to coastal North Carolina to find Charles and Beulah Hunter. The square-jawed Hunter tripled as the Theatre's playwright, stage director and leading man; Beulah, petite and vivacious, was ever the leading lady. In a single afternoon, as Hunter smoked pipe after pipe in the couple's comfortable apartment on board the Theatre, he offered Ms. Ferber, in her words, "a stream of pure gold. . . . Incidents, characters, absurdities, drama, tragedies, river lore, theatrical wisdom poured forth in that quiet flexible voice. He looked, really, more like a small-town college professor lecturing to a backward student than like a show-boat actor."

Having spent four whole days on the Floating Theatre,

and armed with her many notes, Ms. Ferber then naturally retreated to New York, Paris, and the French resort town of St. Jean de Luz to write an "authentic" picture of the American south, throwing the opening narrative back in time and moving it over to the Mississippi River aboard the mythical paddleboat *Cotton Blossom*. The resulting 1926 novel 'Show Boat' comfortably confirmed all of the Southern stereotypes that Northern audiences have insisted on so earnestly for the past hundred years. The story was promptly adapted to a Broadway musical through the genius of Jerome Kern and Oscar Hammerstein, and opened in 1927 to great applause.

❦   ❦   ❦

Red Carroll had a splendid memory and could speak well. His other virtues, according to Charles Hunter, were that he was "loud, easy to see, and looked right." But his mastery of timing and movement, essential to performing on the Floating Theatre's 19-foot-wide stage, was incomplete; and, he was nowhere close to acquiring the chameleon nature required of all talented actors, to feign emotions that he did not feel.

On the Sunday morning that the Floating Theatre arrived in Galesville, Charles Hunter had the sniffles, and by evening had a cough coming on. The following morning, he was living the misery of a full-blown summer cold. It was decided, to Red's great delight and concern, that he would replace Mr. Hunter in that night's play, 'Ten Nights in a Bar Room'. This popular drama charts the declining fortunes of businessman Joe Morgan, who has fallen under the spell of Demon Rum and the evil influence of bar-keeper Simon Slade. It takes the death of Morgan's little daughter Mary, who is hit upside the head by a bottle thrown across the bar, to finally bring Morgan to his senses.

Red spent the afternoon on the stage with Pop Neel, an old trouper with an unlimited supply of patience.

"Let's read it again, son," said Pop. "I'll read Mary and you're Joe, of course."

> MARY: (*Offstage Left.*) Father! Father! Where is my father?
> JOE: (*Raises his head.*) What shame for my child to discover me here again. (*Rises.*)
> MARY: (*Runs in Left. Little Mary is indeed an angel child. She is all that is good and pure in the world and has a forgiving heart. Because this part will probably be played by an adult, she talks in a light voice. She wears a spotless white dress and wears a huge white hairribbon on her head. She sees him and rushes to him.*) Oh, I've found you at last. Now, won't you come home with me?
> JOE: (*Holds her to him.*) Blessings on thee, little one.

"Pop," said Red, "I'm very fond of Mrs. Hunter and she's a terrific actress, but I can't see her playing a girl with a ribbon in her hair."

Pop laughed. "Don't worry about that, Red, she's done this role a hundred times at least. Focus on yourself.

Good thing about this play is that you're a tosspot and drunk for most of it. If you flub a line, the audience will never notice. The thing you can't do is mess up the timing of the other trouper's lines, got it?"

"I've got it, Pop."

"Let's take a break. I think you'll be ready for the full walk-though later this afternoon."

Red took his copy of the script and climbed a hand ladder to the roof of the Theatre. It was one of his favorite spots. It offered a view, a breeze if there was one, and a quiet place to study on a couple of old folding chairs.

He was not alone on the roof. A dozen ring-billed gulls were up there too, enjoying the high perch. They were surprisingly large birds, and stood around with great self-confidence, hardly moving out of the way as Red arranged his chairs. The gulls had been feasting on glass minnows and peanut bunker in neighboring creeks, and were effortlessly laying shocking great piles of guano with a twitch of their tail feathers. One of the gulls came within a few feet of Red, and regarded him with a yellow eye. "You're a brazen fellow," said Red. "Maybe you'd like to hear me read the part of poor old Joe Morgan."

It was not long before Red felt a puff of cooler air on his neck. With his back to the West, and wondering what he would do when Mrs. Hunter, as Mary, threw her arms around his neck—she was pretty old, maybe 40—Red had not seen the rapid development of a wall of blue purple cloud that was sweeping towards Galesville with rain underneath it. The wind suddenly accelerated.

The Floating Theatre had virtues that turned to vices

when the wind came up—you only needed to ask any of the tug's crews. She drafted a mere 14 inches of water empty and had no keel: that's what allowed her to move through water no deeper than a ditch, and to be wrangled and spun round in the little byways where she made port and money. But, it also meant she had a tendency to wander. And, she was very tall for her draft: the two storeys that made such an imposing interior space were to nature just a big surface to push against. So, in a sixty mile an hour wind like the one bearing down on her now, the flat-bottomed barge with the large sail area became the skittish bitch that the tug crews knew her for. She began leaning back on the lines that moored her to the wharf.

Red felt her move and heard the gangway drag a little. There were shouts from below. He rolled his script up and thrust it into his back pocket, and moved the edge of the roofline. The mooring lines holding the Theatre to the wharf looked thin as a pencil now, taking the strain. A couple of troupers were struggling to get a big hawser across to the wharf. "Get on down here, Red!" one of them shouted. Charles Hunter, leaning around the balcony that led to his apartment, looked up at Red and yelled "Watch it, she's going to bust!"

At that moment the forward line snapped and the barge gave a violent lurch. Red, whose anchor foot rested squarely on a slick pile of gull droppings, fell forward. Hunter watched Red somersault from the roof, his head making ringing contact with the upper handrail, his suddenly lifeless body windmilling into the dark water between the barge and the wharf. Hunter was already moving, his eyes glued to the spot where Red went in. Hunter dove, and as the warm water closed over him, he had the absurd thought that he now had another story to tell Edna Ferber.

❧   ❧   ❧

When he awoke from his coma at Johns Hopkins a week later, Red remembered nothing of his fall. He vomited for a day, and would get the spins any time he tried to sit up. But these symptoms, along with a dull headache, soon receded and he was released home.

One lasting effect of his head injury that Red noticed immediately was a vastly improved sense of smell and of taste. This was combined with a craving that he'd never had before. It came to him one day when he was writing a letter of thanks to Charles Hunter for saving his life. Red wanted a crab cake. And he wanted it as soon as possible.

Red spent the fall of 1931 on a nomadic quest throughout Baltimore in search of the perfect crab cake. He had them at Al Kelz's on York Road, at George's Café, at Haussner's on Eastern Avenue, The Spot Diner, The Walker Hasslinger on North Charles Street, and a dozen other places. Some cakes were better than others, but they were all missing some essential spark that he knew was out there.

One late afternoon he was talking to a fish monger down on the waterfront. Red noticed the seagulls waiting expectantly for a fish head or some other morsel, which the man was tossing into the harbor as he cleaned the day's catch.

"Say," asked Red, "does anyone eat seagulls?"

The monger looked at him through a cloud of cigar smoke. "You serious?"

"Yes."

"As a matter of fact they do. They call it different names  at different places. Salt Grouse. White Snipe. Sea Pigeon. Oh yeah, some fancy places called it Bay Cock or Water Pheasant. You order that and you're eating seagull."

"It doesn't seems like there's much meat on them."

"There's only one piece of meat on 'em worth a damn." The man pointed to a passing gull with a long, thin bloody knife. "You see that thing flapping? Well, there's a big muscle in the armpit that pumps that wing. I even know what it's called. The *pectoralis major*."

"And that's edible?"

"If you don't mind a little fish taste to your meat, yeah. Actually kind of a nice piece of white meat. But it's small, you know? And a little fishy."

One afternoon, Red's mother was returning from a lunch with friends and a visit to the market. She was concerned about Randall. He was pale and had dropped a little weight since the accident, and he tired so easily. She wanted him to have another visit with Caleb and Todd, the family doctors, but he kept resisting that. She let herself in the front door. Randall was cooking crabs again. That was another thing, he'd never cared for crab before the accident, and now he was cooking it every day. He'd always been a boy who maybe focused too much on one thing to the exclusion of everything else. She put down her bags, and rounded the door into the kitchen and nearly swooned: there was Randall, with a great meat clever in one raised hand, leaning over an enormous white bird splayed over the counter. There was another giant dead bird—a seagull—laying on the kitchen floor. The horror was really too much. She did swoon.

Later, when she was resting on the settee and the mess in the kitchen had been cleaned up, Red said, "Mother, there's something going on with the biology of gulls. They can live in filthy environments and eat garbage and they're still healthy. Why?"

"I don't know, dear. I really don't know."

"I need to work in an actual kitchen, Mother, a place where I can focus on this dish without having to cook a bunch of other stuff. Not a restaurant of course. Some place else."

🐦   🐦   🐦

Mrs. Carroll visited with the family physicians the following day. Doctors John Caleb and Christopher Todd, who had cared for her through all of her pregnancies, and who had treated Red since infancy, were very attentive. She was a valued client and they were fond of her. And somehow, in this awful economy, her husband was making more money than ever.

"You know Randall," said Mrs. Carroll, "he gets very focused on something and it's hard for him to break off."

"Yes, Patricia, but that's long been a dimension of his personality."

"Perhaps Randall needs to see a psycho-analyst," she suggested.

Caleb and Todd shared a look—they were conservative physicians of the old school. They did not refer patients over to the new Henry Phipps Psychiatric Clinic at Johns Hopkins—unless the patient was crazy. In their opinions, the Hopkins mystique was laid on a little too thick, and they had a low opinion of the emerging "science of the mind." It was a whiff of smoke, subjective and changeable and unserious, a fad. Only the open sewer of fin de siècle Vienna could have first produced and then sustained such a one as Sigmund Freud, with his preposterous ruminations on sex and the subconscious.

And, in practice psycho-therapy had a low entrepreneurial edge to it, serving as something of a jobs program for less skilled persons who could not otherwise find useful employment in the field of medicine. For most patients experiencing depression or anxiety, a quiet weekend in the country, or even better, a half hour divesting one's sins and worries to a priest or minister, could achieve better effects at far less cost than endless sessions with a "therapist." And the patient would be spared the inconvenience of finding his hidey-hole office in some dilapidated neighborhood, and sharing one's secrets with a pretend doctor among his worn furniture, skid-marked carpets, and the remains of his lunch.

"So," said Mrs. Carroll, after hearing this assessment, "you're not very keen on therapy?"

"No, Patrticia, we are not. Closed head trauma like that experienced by your son can have several after effects, most of them completely benign. Randall may have a lesion on the right side of his brain where the impact occurred . . ."

"You mean a scar? On his brain?"

"No, I said a lesion. This can sometimes cause changes in personality, which thankfully has not happened to Randall, and can sometimes create a mild obsession or preoccupation with fine food. The effects may be temporary or permanent."

"What does that mean?"

"It might mean that Randall decides on a career in the restaurant business. He might be very particular about how food is made and presented. But rest assured, he will not be slinging hash over at The White Coffee Pot. It will be fine food that interests him, and nothing else."

"It's all very strange."

"Patricia, it's merely the brain working itself out. We've seen a number of patients with this malady, and heard of several more. We jokingly call it 'Gourmand's Syndrome'. We've thought of writing a paper on it, but cannot take enough time from the practice to amass the evidence."

"Well, I'm worried."

"Don't be. Keep an eye on Randall. He should not do anything strenuous for another six weeks. Then we'll see him again—one of us can come to the house if he won't come here. We're going to give you a twelve ounce bottle of liquid opium. If Randall gets so focused on his project that he stops eating and sleeping properly, a couple of tablespoons should calm him down."

❄   ❄   ❄

Around Christmas, Red learned through a friend that an interesting little club on the Eastern Shore was looking for a cook. It was called the Meridian Club. The pay was negotiable, and the menu was small. It sounded to Red like the perfect place to refine his crab cakes. He called them, "Surf 'N Sky Crab Cakes."

🐟   🐟   🐟

At the Meridian Club, Kathy has finished her round of golf on the back nine losing only three more balls to the water, and by some accident, made a 30-foot putt on the 14th hole. She tallies up her score card—only 132!

In Kathy's estimation, this day with Mrs. Phipps and her friend has gone very well. Like the Club itself, this kind of relationship is new to her—the first steps in the long, delicate negotiations that take place between new brides and the mothers of their husbands.

As they walk to the car, Mrs. Phipps says, "Kathy, I think that it would be very prudent of you to come by here a couple of times each month and enjoy a crab cake sandwich. Since you married my boy John, this place is yours now too, you know. Your name is in the book."

"Mrs. Phipps—Betty—the crab cakes are certainly delicious, but you seem to be making a bigger point and I'd like to know what that is."

Betty smiles and draws closer to her. Quietly, she says,

"Since the day Red Carroll arrived with his crab cake recipe, no member here has died of a heart attack or contracted cancer. No member has suffered dementia, and some of the older folks who looked like they were going that way improved. And more importantly for you, my dear," she says, squeezing Kathy's arm, "no woman at the Meridian has miscarried her child. I've brought all my daughters in law here, and they've all had healthy babies. That recipe is one of the Meridian's best-kept secrets. You understand."

Kathy nods. "I do understand. What's the secret ingredient?"

"You'll figure it out. There's something good in those crab cakes!"

6

Menhaden Burrito Bombs

Springtime in the Tidewater region is as great a miracle to us as it must be to the inhabitants of New England, who winter in their low-ceilinged rooms along frozen streets laboring over righteous political tracts by candle-light, drinking to excess without joy and engaging in self-murder, apparently hating themselves as much as they hate people below the Mason Dixon line whom they have never met.

It is true that our winters along the Chesapeake Bay are not as severe as those along Boston Harbor, the Hudson and East Rivers, and the Delaware—perhaps that explains why our hearts beat with greater warmth than those in Northern breasts.

Yet frosts descend on our countryside too. The Bay itself will sometimes freeze, and snow will fall, enfolding the countryside in a grey, mournful mien. When the brilliant sunshine of April floods our windows, even when accompanied by tumultuous winds, we take special

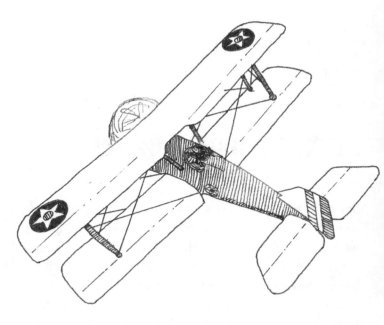

pleasure in knowing that the charms of spring and summer are almost within reach.

Springtime is marked by the welcome return of the field and shed workers who follow the warming sun up the eastern coast of the United States. Known crudely as "fruit tramps," they help growers with the planting and harvesting of the berries, potatoes, and vegetables that load our summer sideboards with delicious fare.

Many field hands are known simply as "Mexicans," though we suspect a fair number of these compact and indefatigable men originate from locales much further south. They manage their sums on little knotted ropes, and refresh themselves with "Kuka Mama," a wad of cocoa leaf mixed with limestone, ash and anise. They will turn a field in nothing but shirtsleeves in a keening, biting wind, and are tireless runners: indeed, before telephone service was regular on the Eastern Shore, they were frequently employed as message carriers between farm and town.

The arrival in the Bay of another migratory workforce, vast schools of *Brevoortia tyrannus*, or Atlantic menhaden, also signal the approach of summer. These most useful of fish are true pelagics, spending their younger years along the continental shelf and entering the Bay in their maturity by the hundreds of millions. They clean the water by filter feeding, and it is enchanting to sit quietly in a boat in an acre-wide patch of menhaden as they graze the surface, sounding nothing but like a gentle rain as they pass.

Menhaden, harmless and smooth, are a critical source of food for many creatures, from the austere osprey to the ruminative striped bass, yet so packed with oil and bones are they that few humans eat them. Indeed, even the Indians appear to have used them only as fertilizer for summer crops, and their name for the fish, *Munnawhatteaug*, translates as "that which manures."

The Mexicans, however, eternally short of cash money and not wishing to eat their wages, have made their peace with the menhaden, and around eventide will cast nets to catch the fish for their large and tightly wrapped burritos, which they call "bombas." This diet has clearly done them no harm at all, judging by the wonderful glow of their skin, brilliant white teeth, and muscled physiques.

As the residents of Cape Charles, Virginia, know, General Billy Mitchell was piloting his single-seat S.E.5a across the Bay on a June afternoon in 1921 when the aircraft's Hispano-Suiza engine threw its propeller, forcing him to crash land in a farm field along King's Creek. He and the young lady accompanying him on the flight—a visiting niece—were uninjured but trapped in the wreckage, which was in danger of catching fire. They were rescued by several Mexican field hands, who had been fishing and cooking their delicious bombas over fires along the shore.

General Mitchell, being very fond of Mexican food, consented to stay for dinner and enjoyed a bomba burrito. Given the tastiness of the meal, and because the bucolic surroundings of Cape Charles were a tonic from the tension and bustle surrounding 'Project B' at Langley field, General Mitchell and his niece were frequent visitors that summer, flying in, having a swim and private nap, and later eating with the workers by their open tents.

General Mitchell often took Mexicans up in his plane for a spin, marveling at their stolidity even in the most daring of maneuvers, and at their resistance to cold and the deprivation of oxygen at higher altitudes. He took to training them to drop large river stones from swooping two-seater airplanes into crab baskets. The Mexicans soon grew so proficient at this trick that he successfully recruited several into the 88th Squadron to drop dynamite, tear gas and bombs on rioting West Virginia miners

94

in the Mingo War, that extraordinary but forgotten event in the late summer of 1921.

This is a faithful representation of how the Mexicans prepare their bomba burritos:

Twenty menhaden, planked and smoked, chiffonade along the shoulder into short strips with a very sharp fillet knife or machete

2 avocados

3 raw eggs

4 bruised tomatoes, diced

1/2 cup cilantro, diced

1/2 onion, diced

1 cup black strap rum

1 handful of sea salt

1 large lemon, juiced

8 flour or corn tortillas

Combine all ingredients in a bowl and then tightly pack into a tortilla. If the ingredients for burritos are unavailable, the menhaden alone can be prepared in the manner described and served in small stacking cups as an amuse-bouche.

Serves 8

7

Lost Boys Oyster Stew

If you wish to smell the sea and nothing else—the sea in its pure, sterling form—you can do no better than to find your way to an oyster house when the haul has been rinsed clean and stands in a great, wet pile on the floor. You may breathe deep and be carried to any place in Neptune's realm. It may soothe you. It might make you giddy. It smells like the first day of creation.

The Northern Neck of Virginia is blessed with a surplus of bent old snaggle-toothed wood frame oyster houses with rough finished boards leaning out over the water on pilings surrounded by mountains of oyster shell. Return in fifty years and you'll find them still, looking ready to fall with the next puff of wind. But for some reason—through northeasters and gales from the west and the occasional hurricane—they don't.

The oyster house on Jackson Creek was not one of those romantic heaps, but was instead a neat white cinder block building with high windows and an inclined concrete floor to drain the catch. It sat at the foot of a well-maintained dock wired for electricity. Alongside the dock was a fifty-foot oyster buy boat named *Bluebell*. She was as trim and ship-shape as the lawn along the creek, and for that matter the house, which was a big place with a wrap-around porch and a red tin roof, surrounded by tall oak trees.

All of this belonged to Tom and Lynne Stanton, a handsome couple in their early thirties. In season, they made the rounds of tongers and dredgers out on Chesapeake Bay, bringing the oysters back here, where their help shucked and steamed them and packed them into gallon cans which were carried on ice to Kinsale. From there, a steamboat might port them north to restaurants, hotels and markets in Alexandria, Washington, Annapolis or Baltimore.

Like other oyster packing businesses, the Stantons had their own brand label printed on their cans. It featured the *Bluebell* with her sail up, bravely cresting a wave and surrounded by seagulls. It read: "Ask for BLUEBELL Hand Packed Deluxe Oysters From Sunny Jackson Creek, Hague Virginia." In smaller bold letters it warned, "KEEP REFRIG-ERATED," and if that were not clear enough, it also read "KEEP ON ICE UNTIL USED."

On occasion Tom and Lynne would pack the *Bluebell* with oysters, lumber and farm produce from the neighborhood, and make a run to ports north. After offloading their cargo, Lynne could shop with the little disposable money they had, and Tom could renew his waterfront acquaintances.

The *Bluebell* was designed for hard work, but she was a good cruising vessel too. She was very stable, with wide open decks and a single mast and boom forward to swing cargo, or to hang a sail if the engine gave out.

Lynne would sit with Tom in the pilot house at the rear of the boat, her arm over his shoulder, watching the shore-line roll past at 12 miles an hour, which was about right for the *Bluebell's* 110 hp Kermath engine. Lynne would take a book to the curved afterdeck behind the pilot house and read in a canvas chair, where the throb of the engine and the splashing of the propeller would lull her to sleep. There were times when she would sit still with her head up and her shoulders forward, her book closed, looking into the middle distance. After seven years of marriage Tom could guess the direction of her thoughts but could not follow her there—who can know the mind of a woman who wants babies that do not come?

Yet Tom had moments of his own. Something from last fall kept coming into his head. He had been working alone on *Bluebell*, crossing the main channel of the Bay in the direction of Bloodsworth Island. He pulled the throttle back to slow ahead and walked forward to even out the load of oysters on deck with a broad shovel. A sudden cold dread came upon him. He looked around, but there were no other boats within miles of his position, and the *Bluebell* was running fine, tracking straight in the flat calm. Then he saw the fin cutting the surface close off the port side. It was a grey black triangle, better than two feet high, and below it was a dark shadow so wide and long that Tom at first thought it was a whale. But the bullet head and submarine shape were all wrong, as was the lazy serpentine swing of its tail. It was almost half the length of the *Bluebell*, casu-ally keeping pace. It rolled slightly and Tom saw its white belly and looked into its great black eye and saw a lower jaw full of tapered, serrated teeth. It held there for a long moment, and then turned smoothly away and was gone. Later, Tom came to think of that shark as representing time itself: hunting always, silently tracking a man through his life, enormous and without mercy. Perhaps, he thought, the only thing that could defeat it was one's own child.

On a late April afternoon in 1930, Tom was guiding the *Bluebell* around the corner of the sandbank that separated Jackson Creek from the open Potomac, and saw a tall figure standing on his dock. It was his younger brother Ken, in worn Red Wing boots, faded jeans, an open shirt under a dusty leather jacket and a travel bag at his feet, a pair of green Willson motorcycle glasses perched on his nose. Like Tom, he was a waterman, but of a different kind.

"You're back," said Tom.

"I'm back."

"You hungry, Ken?"

"I am."

"Well," said Tom, "you can help me clear these oysters and get your appetite up, then we'll eat."

At dinner, Lynne made a fuss over Ken, giving him double servings of mashed potatoes, gravy and chicken. In return, Ken had stories and treasures from the road. He was a hard-hat diver whose trade took him to out of the way spots like Veracruz, Honduras, Anegada, Bermuda, Vero Beach, the Florida Keys and Port Royal. He'd just finished a project off Padre Island, where the beaches harbored rattlesnakes and cattle with horns six feet across.

"I brought you this, Lynne," said Ken, pushing a velvet drawstring bag across the table.

"Ohhh, gold?"

"No, better than that. Be careful opening it."

Lynne looked inside. "What is this red dust?"

"It's not dust. It's spice. Got it from a Creole man in a place called Port Mansfield. Dip your finger in there and give it a taste."

"It's good," she said. "I can taste paprika and clove. I think there's nutmeg and pepper in there too."

"The man said there were fourteen spices in it, and that you could put it over any kind of seafood. I figured that it might liven up your oyster stew."

"Liven up my oyster stew! Tom, did you hear what your brother just said?"

"I did," said Tom. It was an old joke. Lynne's oyster stew was superb, and Ken ate vast quantities of it, but he enjoyed teasing her about possible improvements.

"Now, Lynne," Ken said, with a thoughtful air, "there are perhaps a hundred ways to make oyster stew, am I right?"

"Yes, it seems everyone has their own way of going about it."

"But there is a danger common to them all, is there not?"

"The only way to mess up an oyster stew is to overcook the oysters. They get rubbery if you're not paying attention."

"Precisely. So the cooking process should be shortened to prevent that. You put butter in your stew, no?"

"Of course. Four tablespoons."

"And you put in milk, too?"

"Yes—two cups."

"Well, if you are already using butter and milk together, why not just use buttermilk and save some time?"

Lynne's jaw dropped in mock astonishment. "What?"

"And another thing. You add potatoes to your stew."

"Yes."

"You also add oyster crackers to it—why?"

"To thicken it."

"A true innovator would replace both those ingredients with potato chips!" Ken proclaimed, slapping the table. They had a good laugh at that.

Over coffee and pie, Tom asked, "How long are you going to be with us, Ken?"

"I'm thinking for the summer, if that's alright with you two. My sinuses were acting up diving that Texas wreck. It's time for a break."

"You are welcome to stay as long as you like," said Lynne, smiling, "if you agree to stay away from my kitchen with your innovations and whatnot."

"I promise," said Ken, with a grin. "Say, Tom, are you going to keep up the family tradition and build a boat or two this summer for some extra money?"

"I was thinking about it. Got plenty of seasoned wood, for it, anyway."

"When was it we made those Jenkins Island crab scrapes?"

"That was three years ago," said Tom.

"You all should make those again," said Lynne, "they were pretty. And they sold fast too."

"It's a good little deadrise skiff for sail or power," said Tom. "Leo Bassett put an outboard on his, and I'm certain I saw another one of them gaff-rigged passing by on the river not long ago."

"Well," said Ken, "I've got an idea for getting us some help. I hitched a ride in today with Joe Friedl. You know him?"

"The fella that runs the poor farm? Yeah, I think we've met."

"He told me that this depression has got so bad that some single parents—most of them war widows—can't take care of their kids and are dropping them off at the poor farm. But Friedl's not really set up to take care of children, it's more for older folks with no family. They're supposed to grow their own food there, you know, and Friedl says that it's hard to manage kids in the field and to see to their schooling. And they're noisy. And they cry a lot."

"I'll bet they do," said Tom, thinking about the farm, a stark place that sat just off the state road with a potter's field behind it where the destitute, the old, the sick, the forgotten—whether white, black, Indian or immigrant, no matter—were buried in plain pine boxes in unmarked graves with no ceremony and no one to mourn them.

"Friedl's trying to place some of the youngsters that he's got over there. As an elected 'Overseer of the Poor' as he put it, he has authority from the government of Virginia to bind youngsters out to homes with decent people."

"Bind them? What does that mean?"

"I guess it's some kind of contract. You give a youngster

room and board and take care of his education, get some work out of him, and at age twenty-one, you send him on his way with fifty dollars and something useful, like a horse or livestock if you're a farmer, or maybe a boat if he's going to make a living on the water."

"And you're thinking we ought to have one of these children here?" asked Tom.

"No, I'm thinking two. Friedl told me he has two brothers there who are sharp as tacks."

"How old are they?"

"Twelve and fourteen, he said."

"Good Lord. What use would they be making boats?"

"We can always use extra hands, you know that. They can fetch things, or set clamps to start. And then we can teach them some basic skills, planing, sanding, making trunnels, things like that."

"Well, I don't want to sign any kind of contract or have teenagers I don't know ranging around here," said Tom. "Lynne, you've been awfully quiet. What do you think?"

"Maybe," she said, "Mr. Friedl would be satisfied with having the boys work here over the summer. And when we get back to oyster packing in the fall, the boys can return to the farm."

"Where would they stay?"

"We can set them up in the back of the oyster house," said Lynne. "You know something, Tom? Your father, God rest his soul, would have approved. He liked teaching young people how to make small boats."

Tom thought a moment and nodded, "Yes, he did. But he would also look to the business end of it and ask whether it made sense. Let's try it out for a few weeks and see if it works. If it doesn't, the kids go back to the farm."

🐞   🐞   🐞

After dinner, Tom opened his father's chests of boat-building tools, which by themselves were a kind of monument to the craft. Here were dozens of gleaming Buck Brothers slick chisels wrapped in oiled sailcloth. Timber framers, beveled, double-beveled, mortised, stubby, wide, tall, they did many of the complex jobs needed to frame and plank a boat. There were hand saws, a broad axe that was easily 150 years old, maul hammers and caulking mallets, riveting tools, bare-footed ship augers for drilling deep holes, a spokeshave, bullnose, rabbet and round-bottom planes to smooth timbers and frames, and scores of plain iron clamps to hold beams, planks and frames together.

Tom and Ken's late father was a boat builder who thoroughly understood the properties of oak, elm, pine and spruce, the utility of different hull designs, and the dynamic stresses that wind and water had on small craft. He was what they call a "rack of eye" builder, so veteran that he relied more on intuition than he did written plans. In a land where many built "backyard boats," he was something of a sage, and it was not unusual to see a waterman—the most independent, tough, prideful and stubborn kind of man that God ever created—asking him to "come have a look" at a build to make sure it was going right.

"It's just parts that need putting together," their father would say with a half smile, knowing that he was talking a bit of nonsense. The wood going into his creations needed to be worthy of the trust, and he would look into the surface of a piece, run his hand down the grain and rap it with his knuckles or a maul, listening to the sound that came out of it for dryness, sappiness or other character defects. It was either completely right or it was wrong. To him, well made boats were art, pure and simple, the most useful art ever created by mankind, that could carry souls out into the absolute wilderness and bring them safely home, and look beautiful doing it. And a poorly built boat? Why, it was a false promise and a lie that on the right day could get a man killed.

❦ ❦ ❦

The brothers who came over from the poor farm were named Christian and Jack. Tom and Ken showed them where they would build, a flat area below the trees and bordering the creek. Shipwrights had used the spot in colonial days to build coastal trading sloops, and in a low spring tide or a blowout one could still make out several massive timbers they had fixed to the creek bed, allowing large vessels to slide into the water on their keels.

"Boys," said Tom, gesturing to a large pile of lumber, "this is where we are going a build a 22-foot modified Hooper Island sharpie, which is a single-masted crabbing and gunning skiff that will fetch a good price."

The boys stared at him.

"Do either of you know any math?"

"We were taught to cipher to the rule of three," said Christian.

"That should be helpful. Have you ever worked on boats?"

"No sir," said Jack, "but we know how to swim. We don't want to go back to the farm. There's a lady there who has a doll she talks to. And everyone's sad."

"What Jack's trying to say is that we are glad to be here and will help any way we can," said Christian.

"If we go back to the farm they'll have us planting radishes in the noonday sun with a bunch of old folk!" said Jack.

"Alright," said Ken. "We'll teach you a little boat building as we go. It's a very useful set of skills. You'll get the hang of it if you pay attention and follow instructions."

❧   ❧   ❧

The boys were mystified by the lofting or laying down process which converted Tom's paper plans for the sharpie to full-sized parts, but they proved useful for the eternal labor of sanding and fabricating wooden pins or trunnels to hold the sharpie together.

Tom offered them boat-building truisms—"You can't ever have enough plain old iron clamps"—and the occasional lecture: "Take a look at this log. We're not going to use the bark, right? And, we're not going to use the inch inside the bark either, because that's where the sap flowed in this tree. It's called heart wood, and it's weaker than the other wood. No, what we want is the wood at the center, which we cut straight across for strength. The more growth rings a tree has, the finer the wood. So, we want to be careful picking out the logs that we use, and we should know how we're going to use them in constructing the vessel."

Tom also said, smacking a stick into his palm, "Every good boat starts with this, the king of wood, white oak. A beautiful color. A fine grain. Very hard, very durable. Holds a pin like nothing else. Can be used almost anywhere you want precision and strength. In the keel, in the stem, in the frames, the floors, you name it. Bends easy when you steam it. We'll be doing a lot of work with it."

It took three days to construct the sharpie's keel, bow stem, centerboard trunk and sternpost, which didn't look like much of anything to the boys. However, once the planks were steamed, bent and fastened in place along the frames, the boys could see the shape of the hull, and appreciate the sharpie's elegant and fast lines. And they got to know those lines very well because they spent many hours sanding the hull smooth.

Looking over their work, Ken told them, "This, boys, is how you gain immortality. You build a beautiful boat that can run fast and look good, you'll never be alone. If you can make sailing yachts, why, wealthy people will come to you on their knees. They will want your art. You see, rich people use their boats to make a statement to their friends and to the world. People you don't even know will know *your* name. And people not even born yet will step on board a craft built by you and will love what you have made, long after you've moved on to your just rewards."

"And Christian, as a young man you should remember

something important," added Ken.

"What?"

"Pretty girls like pretty boats. It's a natural law."

It was a good life for the boys. They were up at dawn, ate a hearty breakfast at Lynne's table, were up to their elbows in sawdust amid the noise of hammering and sawing, had sandwiches for lunch, were back on the sharpie for a few hours and then free to swim in the creek or to fish from the Stanton's rowboat, finishing the day with dinner back up in the house.

"Tom, we've never built a boat this quickly," said Ken one evening.

"You're right, this sharpie's been quick. All we need to do now is get on the spars and do the finishing. I'm thinking a nice satin white paint with primer mixed in. Then we got to go over to Bobby Wood's place and get him to cut us a couple of sails."

"If we had more hands, we could turn this into a regular production line," said Ken. "Who knows how many we could turn out before oyster season?"

"I was thinking the same thing," said Tom. "Christian, do you think some of the other boys at Mr. Friedl's farm would be helpful making boats?"

"Yes, sir. They'd do anything to get off that farm," said Christian.

"How many are there?"

"Five. Nick, Will, Mike, Alex, and Jeremy. There's also an orphan boy named Keith, but he doesn't count."

"Why is that?"

"He's only five or six years old. He still sucks his thumb."

Tom looked at Lynne. She said, "We can't leave the little boy there by himself. So if the rest of them come, he must come too."

"All right, let's go back over to the farm tomorrow and talk with Mr. Friedl."

By the middle of June, the 'Stanton Boatyard', as Ken was jocularly calling it, had completed four Hooper Island sharpies. Tom and Ken were proud of the work. Tom's intent to produce numerous copies of a single type of vessel was guided by thrift alone: there was no need to spend money and time on new boat plans; it was cheap to use and reuse the same custom templates, moulds and strongback on which the boats were shaped; and the tempo of each new build was all the faster for having done it before.

For the boys, repeat builds lifted much of the fog between the theory and practice of laying down a small boat. The swirl of arcane terms—"king post," "hackmatack," "stop water" or "centerboard trunk log" grew less mystifying, and several boys were willing to swear on a stack of bibles they understood Ken when he said, "We'll next mortise the frames to make the oak chines flush and notch them for the oak deck clamps." The boys now referred to themselves as "apprentice shipwrights" with a level of seriousness that did not escape the Stantons.

One afternoon as they ate a lunch of peanut butter and jelly sandwiches, Tom announced, "Boys, we've nearly used up all of our seasoned wood and we've spent our last penny out of the build fund for paint, rigging and sails. It's time to get some money out of these sharpies so we can keep going."

"Where are we going to sell them?" asked the boys.

"There are boat yards and clubs on the western shore that might know of some buyers. We'll tow the sharpies up there behind the *Bluebell*."

"Who gets to go?" asked Christian.

"Everyone's worked real hard and we can all use a little break for a few days, so everyone goes," said Tom. There was a general cheer—a real sea cruise! "Christian, I'll count on you to make sure the boys have some bedding. You boys will also want a change of clothes for the trip. We'll leave tomorrow morning."

As they cruised north the next day, Tom decided to put in at Solomon's Island to talk with Clarence Davis at the M.M. Davis & Son Shipyard. "Davis made a bunch of tugs for the war effort," he explained to Ken, "and now he's into big yachts, but he might know somebody in the area looking for a little sharpie."

Davis was intrigued at the sight of the *Bluebell* leading a flotilla of sharpies into Mill Creek, and met them at his wharf.

"Stanton, is it? I knew your father. And I've opened more than one can of your oysters. Now who are these fellows?"

he asked, gesturing at the boys, who were manning the ropes to the sharpies bobbing alongside the wharf.

Tom turned and looked at the boys as though seeing them for the first time. Lynne had packed each of them a clean, pressed shirt and pair of shorts for walking around town, but that was for later—right now the boys were still dressed in their ill-fitting, dirty work clothes, and to Tom they resembled street urchins. But most stood with their backs straight and their feet wide, and a couple had their arms crossed and heads tilted, appraising Mr. Davis and his magnificent boat yard, which was nothing at all like the little hollow where they worked, but they would not be intimidated. "Watch the damn paint, Mike," one of them said in an undertone, as a sharpie bumped the dock.

Davis understood their mood immediately. He knew it well.

"You boys built these boats, didn't you?" he asked. They nodded. "Well, let's have a look." Davis climbed aboard two of the sharpies checking for balance, fit and finishing. He addressed Tom and Ken but made sure the boys could hear him. "They are tight boats and sturdy. Very nice craftsmanship. If you want to leave these two with me, I should be able to find buyers for them right quick. Now, we're busy today but if your team wants a tour I'll show them a bugeye that we're building for a client. He's calling it the *Pandora III* and means to race it up in New England."

❦   ❦   ❦

After leaving the Davis yard the boys were lounging in the sun on the deck of the *Bluebell* as she cruised along the Maryland shore past Calvert Cliffs and Parker's Creek.

"Say, did you hear what Mr. Davis called us," remarked Alex, "he said we were a team."

"We are a team," said Nick. "Maybe we should have an official name. We could call ourselves the 'Bay Scouts'.

"We'd need a motto," added Christian. "How about, 'Have a Plan!' Or maybe, 'Learn About the Sea and About Business!'"

"That's a little corny," said Will, after a pause.

"What's corny mean?"

"That means it's goofy."

"We're like Tootles and Nibs," announced Keith.

"Who are they?"

"They're Lost Boys. Mrs. Stanton has been reading me a story about Peter Pan. They are boys whose parents have gone missing. We're like them."

"If the parents are missing doesn't that mean they're the ones who are lost?" asked Jeremy.

"Parents can't get lost. Boys can get lost," said Keith. "That's what the story says."

"Ok, Keith." said Christian. "Maybe Lost Boys is a good name for who we are."

It was a breezy day with light chop out of the northwest, and when *Bluebell* was opposite West River she came across a regatta of small sailboats racing between red and green cans. They were small twenty-foot sloops carrying lots of sail and were heeled well over. One of them came quite close, her sharp bow throwing spray down her side under an immaculate expanse of sail. A tanned young man in a white tennis shirt at the tiller was saying something clever to two girls who sat laughing on the edge of the cockpit. The blond one was pulling the hair from her face and her eyes locked on Christian's for an instant as they sped past. Christian looked down at his worn, paint-smeared khakis and blown-out sneakers and felt impossibly low.

"Ken, let's go into West River and talk with Dick Hartge," said Tom. "He knows everybody and maybe he'll have an idea where we can sell these sharpies."

Captain Hartge gave the boys sodas and had nice things to say about the sharpies, but suggested they go up to Annapolis or cross over to St. Michaels to find buyers.

"Now Tom," he said, "things are tough for most people right now, but I think they're going to get better and when they do, small class boat racing is going to take off. There's even a couple of young fellows thinking of starting a new club here. They call it the OODYC—Our Own Damned Yacht Club!"

Hartge handed Tom a carved half model of a round-bottomed sloop. "I like the idea of a Chesapeake Twenty Class, and that hull design should be just about right for racing."

"It's a beauty," said Tom, holding it up in the light of the shop. "You have plans you can share?"

"Well . . . I'll tell you what, Tom. I'll give you a couple of minutes to draw from that model and if you can write fast I'll quote the offsets for you and the rest you can figure out pretty easy."

"That's generous of you, thanks Cap'n."

"No problem. The OODYC is talking about running a regatta for 20s at the end of the summer—probably Labor

Day—and you might want to put something together for that. With all these boys, looks like you already got a crew!"

⚓ ⚓ ⚓

The Stantons found buyers for the two remaining sharpies on Spa Creek in Annapolis and in celebration took the boys on a foot tour and candy-buying excursion. June Week had finished so they were deprived of the sight of midshipmen in their dress whites walking the street, but there were shops with photographs and postcards of Mids in their glorious uniforms.

One shop was selling white tennis shirts for the startling price of four dollars apiece. Christian thought about it long and hard—four dollars was half of his cut from the sale of the sharpies—but bought one anyway.

In the sun, wearing their town clothes, coins rattling in their pockets and eating the fruits of their labor in the form of Zagnuts and Valomilk Candy Cups, the boys felt prosperous and whole. There was a glow about the day that marked a change in fortune for the boys, a kind of bouyant hope and confidence that remained with them for a long time.

Keith had insisted on buying himself a pack of Wax Lips, which replaced his thumb for a little while, but then he began chewing the wax, which was delicious, and then made the mistake of swallowing a big lump of it, which gave him a stomach ache. Tom carried him back to the *Bluebell* on his shoulder.

❦ ❦ ❦

With the *Bluebell* free of her train of sharpies, Tom steered her south and gave the boys a turn at the helm. Ken set up a small charcoal grill and made a waterman's stew in a deep frying pan, with bacon, diced onions, potatoes, celery and—of course—tinned oysters.

Night came on and Ken draped old army blankets over the sleeping forms on deck, and walked back to the wheelhouse where Tom pulled a couple of cigars from his shirt pocket.

"Have a smoke, Ken."

"Hoyo de Monterrey? Now that's living high."

"It's been a good trip."

"Yes it has." They smoked and watched the moon pull itself up from the distant line of the eastern shore. "Tom, I've been thinking. Between making sharpies I think we should set up another strongback and see if we can loft a modified version of that racing boat that Captain Hartge shared with you. That round bottom hull might be a little tricky, but if we get the boys involved they'll have a boat of their own."

"Are you thinking they could come back up here to race on Labor Day?"

"Yes, I am."

"Alright. I think it might be good to expose the boys to the glamour of an Annapolis regatta. It's not my world, but that's not to say it's the wrong world for the boys."

"A good boat can take you places," said Ken, nodding at the moon, "yes it can."

8

Ye Corne Hole Cakes

Among our circle of good friends who enjoy the beauty of the Tidewater and the pleasure of fresh local food is the Preservation Surrogacy Manager of the British Library. Each summer, she escapes her London offices for travel and sunshine. She is a frequent guest on our Tartan 5300, and joined us one afternoon for a languid sail to a quiet anchorage on the Chester River. Before taking the launch into town for dinner at the Black Swan Tavern, we enjoyed a glass of chilled sangria on the afterdeck.

Our guest was captivated by the farms along the river and the neat rows of corn growing almost to the water's edge. The corn reminded her, she said, of a curious old document that the Library staff had discovered when it purchased several notebooks containing Sir Arthur Conan Doyle's first novel, *The Narrative of John Smith*.

The novel was never published—Sir Arthur later claimed it was lost in the mails en route to his publisher—but it was evident that he had done a great deal of research, as his notebooks were crammed with rare original documents about Smith's expedition to Virginia.

Remarkably, each of the old documents in Sir Arthur's notebooks bore the stamp *Museum Britannicum*, marking them as property of the British Library. A quick search of the card catalog archives by the Library staff contained an enigmatic entry about these very documents: "Virginia Colony maps & miscellany. Mr. Doyle relates destroyed in underground railway ex'plosn 30 October 1883."

Folded neatly between the pages of one of Sir Arthur's notebooks was an affidavit dated May 21, 1610, which was addressed to the Virginia Company in London by three angry men from Cornwall who demanded reparations, back pay and lost income from the Company. The men swore "on all that is holie and before ourre great Godde" that Captain Smith had lured them to the colony under false pretenses and abandoned them to the Indians in one of his forays up the James River to find food in the cruel winter of 1607.

Theirs was not the first complaint made against Captain Smith, nor was it the last.

      ☙   ☙   ☙

These days we tend to think of Captain John Smith as essentially ours, though he was very much the Briton: like many of his countrymen he ventured to the Americas, stayed a short time, and then returned home to make a living writing about the experience.

Smith was only 27 years old when he set foot in Virginia in April 1607. He would stay for 30 tumultuous months, and sail home in October 1609 following a freak accident in which his gunpowder pouch caught a stray spark and blew a great hole in his leg, almost ending his life.

Most of the leadership of the Virginia colony—older and of better blood—disliked Captain Smith intensely. He was too free with his opinions, and too confident in his own good looks, excellent mustaches, and physical prowess. They marked him as a social climber and upstart who threatened the Virginia venture. They were wrong only on the last point. Smith's military discipline and capacity for violence were essential to the colony's survival in its early days. He was the first of the Indian

fighters, cuffing, booting, stabbing and shooting representatives from several local tribes in much the same way he had beheaded, shot and stabbed numerous Turks in his youth. In this way he secured food and a wary respect from the indigenous peoples.

◄◙► ◄◙► ◄◙►

But to return to our guest from the British Library. She made the wonderful point over our dinner in Chestertown that "the New World was, and is, about corn!" When she shared that the 1610 affidavit contained a recipe for a kind of corn cake, we insisted that she must share a copy, which she has kindly done. We reprint relevant portions of it below.

Me lord Sir Thomas Smythe,

Wee three are cousins and tin miners
of uncommon skille from the villege of
Twelvesheads in the hamlet of Todpool. In
the falle of 1606 a Captain John Smithe
came into our countrie saying that he
needed stronge men who knewe howe to
find golde in the New Worlde. As wee have
already said, wee have greate skille at locat-
ing mettals of all kindes, be it golde duste,
nougats, or veins deepe in the earthe, using
the Spanish dipping needle for thee pur-
pose, but also using ourre eyes and braynes
together, which we call "the syance of
deduction."

The mentioned Captain Smithe tolde us
the New Worlde was fulle of golde, and that
hee would like us to join the venture, and
that alle neceesaries would be provided for
oure comforte and sustainement while wee
mined. To oure newwe sorrow we assented
and after horride months in a smelle and
leakee vessell with mouldy foode and a sicke
companiee, wee landed only to finde the
same conditions on lande, but now with
snakkes, bugges, straynge beasts and ras-
callie heathens who stolle our provender,
clothes, and even the lives of our frynds.
Finding the coastalle soyale of Virgina to be

spumy sandie and useless
forre golde, we implored
Smithe to takke us up the
varrious rivers and freshets
for bettere grounde, but
the companiee coming shortte of foode as
winter descended wee were forced into expe-
ditions trading with yee savages or stealynge
their maize and dryed meets.

On the faytal daye with Smithe a large
partee of indyans killed every man of our partee excepting us and Smith. Wee were then
in countrie belonging to the indyan head
manne who called himself Powhatan. Wee
were dragged into the cyrcle of his villege
to dye, and as indyan men were to crushhe
Smithe's hedde between two big rockes he
cryed out to Powhatan that his life should
be spared and that we three cousins should
be made slaves in exchange for his libertee.
Beforre we could protest, Powhatan's dusky
daughter Pohantas came and threwwe her
arms around us saying thatte wee were hers
and being a coying maidde and much loved
by her people, wee were giv'n over to her and
her frynds who were likewise young lithe
tawny maiddes and wyse in ways that are
notte Christian. And soo they used us over
long monthhes as their closest friendes.

The winter being harshe, and the exterions

of our service to our Indian mistresses making us most hungry, we survived only by making cakkes of corne or as the savages call it maize. And wee made it in this way: banking a largge fire in a kind of pitt encircled by stone, we took a wide stick or stonne and made a holle in the hot embers, into which we packed an admixture of corne meale made pliable with grease from beaver, muskratt or deere. After this cooked to browning, we then stucke a narrowe stick into it and ate it off the stick while hotte. The Indians at first laughed at this contryvance or food, which we called corne hole cakes, but themselves soone experimented by cooking the admixture around venison, which they called corne dogges.

[*We omit this part of the affidavit that narrates the cousins' "escape" from the Indians, though it appears more likely the young Indian ladies let them go after what can only be described as a fascinating cultural exchange*].

Forre breachhe of contracte, the losse of oure time thatte wee would have putte to bettere use, forre our suffering and sorrowe, wee demand of you 25 gold Unites per manne.

[SIGNED]
John Holmes
Sherlocke Holmes
James Holmes

9

The Original Floater's Stew

The Jefferson Islands Club was founded by several senior Senate Democrats in 1931. The Club was located on Poplar Island at the mouth of the East Bay, just off Tilghman Island and a short ride from the town of St. Michael's. They built there a lovely white clubhouse, which contained eleven bedrooms and even a Presidential Suite. A popular retreat for members of all three branches of government, the clubhouse burned down in 1946, for reasons unknown.

Given its exclusive membership, the by-laws of the Club firmly prohibited reporters and indeed record-keeping of any kind. There was a single exception: the popular annual New Year's Eve address, which was always directly transcribed by the Clerk of the Supreme Court of the United States, in his own hand.

A fragment of a New Year's Eve address was recovered from the burned remains of the clubhouse on Poplar Island at some point in the 1940s. It is undated, but is signed by Clerk of Court Charles Elmore Cropley, who filled that position from 1927 to 1952. The speaker is unknown, but he appears to have served in the First World War. He is a man of rough language and rougher sentiments, and we have considered editing his remarks on this fascinating recipe, but have decided *custodiens omnia eadem* is the better course.

"... finished the weekend in Paris exhausted and penniless and had to see the medico for months afterwards to pay Venus her wages but as you can imagine it was worth every bit of it!
[Long laughter.]
"We then decamped for Compiègne and during the couple of days there I had the chance to ride about with several of my staff and happened on a kind of bistro in the tiny hamlet of Saint-Jean-Aux-Bois. It was there I learned more in a single afternoon about the French manner of cooking than I learned in the next six months in Paris as we labored over that damned treaty.
"The man running the place did not expect us, of course, but when we showed up he uncorked a bottle, hustled out to the garden and before our very eyes began plucking snails off the stonework, which he threw by the handful into a boiling pot. His daughter pulled down a couple of ducks from a rafter, dressed them and placed them in a bowl with honey, crushed sage, lavender and basil. This was all done with great economy and no fuss, and in under an

hour we were enjoying the best provincial cooking I ever had.

"It occurred to me the French were on to something. Only they have the audacity to take what any of us would call poor man's food, dress it up fancy, and eat it. Think of it: grab a frog hopping around the neighborhood, throw some fine butter on it in a pan, call it 'cuisses de grenouilles' and charge us Army men four francs a plate!

[Laughter. Senator ----- takes ill and is removed from the room.]

"The Frenchman looks no further than his back yard and asks what he can eat out of it. We can apply that same spirit of thrift here. I have seen you fellows with your rods and reels spend hours trying to catch some of those damned rockfish, which seem to me the moodiest fish I've ever met—all hot and ready to go one minute and the next sulking on the bottom for hours or days. Remember last summer when General [inaudible] did us the courtesy of bringing to the Club some cases of grenades. Now, that made fishing easy and also amusing, but there is an even easier way to put fish on the table.

[Congressman ----- takes ill and is carried from the room, followed by Senator -----.]

"The population of fish in the Bay, like any other population of living creatures, experiences its own mortality due to accident or disease. These fish then rise to the surface, where they are clearly visible and easy to net. The watermen here call them "floaters.""

"On any given day you can scoop three or four from the water and put them in a bucket. Some might protest that a desiccating, stinking, eyeless striped bass which has been for-aged on by birds and perhaps crabs is not proper for human consumption, but when packed in road salt and Bay mud and cooled for several hours, their flesh undergoes a curious conversion, and they become delightful base for a stew. Throw some dry white wine into a pot with two teaspoons of olive oil, add tomatoes, garlic cloves, clam juice and chopped parsley, and there you are!

[Loud objections from the assembly.]

"Well yes as a matter of fact that is the very stew you enjoyed this evening, but gentlemen please. . . ."

The fragment of the New Year's Eve address ends here. Unfortunately, because the speaker did not give specific metes and measures for his recipe, we must leave it to the intrepid reader of this cookbook to determine them herself. If you do attempt this recipe, please notify the Society of the results.

10

Bay Hundred Bootloaf

Tilghman Island on the Chesapeake Bay is a charming location at any time of year, but those of us who love cooking have found Columbus Day weekend in early October to be an excellent time to gather at an old ship captain's home backed up on Harris Creek to savor the fruits of the season, and to cook. There are usually six to eight of us. Some of the names you might recognize include five star chefs from New York City, Washington, D.C., and Philadelphia.

In past years, we have enjoyed selecting a variety of recipes from a charming cookbook that we found in an old bureau drawer, *From a Lighthouse Window*. From corn-frites to crab cakes to a dozen varieties of oyster stew, we have "rediscovered" some classic island recipes, each a testament to the culinary skills of Tilghman residents over the past two hundred years.

Tilghman Island has a fascinating history. Native Americans fished and hunted here (it is thought that Paw Paw Cove may be one of the oldest human settlements in North America). European settlers arrived in the 1600s, planting crops in the rich sandy soil and raising livestock. Slavery was unfortunately legal in Maryland, and many African-Americans in servitude here contributed to the history (including the culinary history) of the Island.

The Island was also the scene of various conflicts in the early history of the United States. During the Revolutionary War, the Island was threatened by British naval forces. The Continental Congress ordered the Island natives to remove their livestock to the mainland so that raiding parties could not re-supply British forces. The British were back in the War of 1812, and occupied the Island for a brief time.

One of the favorite foods of our pastry chefs—which we create each year—is the Bay Hundred Bootloaf.

The origins of this recipe are obscure. It is thought that Hessian soldiers living among the Tilghman Island

population brought the recipe with them, and that the Tilghman Island ladies, always quick to pick up on a good thing, quickly adapted the recipe with their own inimitable style.

Our old cookbook (we have the 1898 first edition printing) explains that Hessian soldiers (who were German mercenaries in the employ of the British Army) often had to march great distances in a single day and would get ahead of the supply wagons that were supposed to feed them. While they could forage for food among the lush fields and orchards of the Chesapeake Bay region, they had great difficulty obtaining fresh bread to nourish them.

This gave rise to the Bootloaf. The Germans wore tall black leather boots that retained heat and moisture long after their exhausted owners had taken them off after a day's march. After setting up their tents for the evening, the Hessians would take four handfuls of flour (sometimes mixed with ground corn), a small tin cup of water, and a pinch of  ground edelweiss flower (which acts as a leavening and flavoring agent), knead the ingredients together, and place the dough deep into the still warm and still moist boot.

To ensure that the dough would rise and harden over-night, the Germans would place their tall miter caps or forage caps overtop the boot. In the morning, a soldier would use the bayonet from his rifle to spear the Bootloaf, bake it over the coals, and eat it with honey and butter, when available.

Hessian soldiers were feared by Continental soldiers of the early United States, in part because they could show up anywhere, at any time. It is thought that the Hessian's remarkable forced marches—they were known on one occasion, the Battle for Jon's Forge, to have marched 350 soldiers 32 miles in a single day—can be credited to the sustainment offered by the Bootloaf.

These days, of course, the recipe does not call for the use of a black leather boot. It still remains a fun and historic dish to create, and is delicious on a cool fall evening with a stew or soup, or with coffee on a Sunday morning, with the sun coming up over the creek.

Notes and Comments

Smith Island 21-Layer German Chocolate Cake

Because there is no way to validate this story's description of the movements of the U-1105 in the closing days of WWII, it's best to believe the accounts of the British and U.S. navies as to how she eventually came to rest on the bottom of the Potomac River. The *Black Panther* was a remarkable vessel for her time, and it's a shame the Navy sunk her instead of putting the boat on display for generations to enjoy.

A queer wrinkle concerning the final resting-place of the *Black Panther* is explained by Maryland archeologists on a State website: "An error in the [Navy's] transcription of longitude and latitude figures masked [the U-boat's actual] location for decades until the transposition of the figures was discovered and sport divers relocated the vessel" in 1985.

Diving on the U-1105 is unpleasant: she's in deep water with a current and visibility is very limited. If you lose contact with the wreck, you're in a black-green limbo and it's best to simply return to the surface.

Other shipwrecks of historical significance are nearby, including the *Tulip*, a Union gunboat from the Civil War which killed nearly every man on board when she blew a boiler in November, 1864.

The story otherwise appears to accurately describe advanced communications technologies on board U-boats. While the *Regenbogen* order issued by B.d.U was promptly countermanded by headquarters after it was issued, some captains chose to scuttle or disable their submarines, while others surrendered them whole.

Croaker on a Stick

While I am unable to locate any reference to "Leroy Leroy" in the *Maryland Gazette* records at my disposal, or to the cholera epidemic of 1832 being associated with a youth selling fish on a stick, this account contains many interesting facts, among them the comparative differences between English and American horse-racing.

Modern analysts of the 1832 cholera outbreak in New York City observe that "most of the victims drew their water from a public pump on Broad (now Broadwick) Street. An infected baby's diapers had been dumped into a cesspool near the well." For more, read *How Epidemics Helped Shape the Modern Metropolis* by John Noble Wilford in the New York Times of April 15, 2008.

Cholera remains deadly even today. The United Nations is currently trying to avoid liability for 8,000 dead and 700,000 sickened in Haiti following the UN's deployment of "peacekeepers" to the island in 2010, who scientists believe introduced the disease there.

The New York civic leader who remarked that only "intemperate dissolute & filthy people" were getting sick was merchant and philanthropist John Pintard (1759-1844). We should not judge him too harshly, as his comments were made in a private letter to his daughter; further, without him, we would not have Santa Claus, because his promotion of St. Nicholas as the patron saint of New York City prompted Washington Irving to create the fat, jolly man with the clay pipe we celebrate today.

Hog Island Pork Tenderloins

"Across two centuries, the distilling of whiskey from rye grain was an important Maryland industry." So says historian James H. Bready, writing in the *Maryland Historical Magazine* in 1990. In the years leading up to Prohibition, Maryland was generating over five million gallons of whiskey annually, behind Kentucky and Pennsylvania. Much of the industry was located in Southern Maryland, where portions of this story unfold.

In 2014, the Slow Food Foundation for Biodiversity added Hog Island figs to its "Ark of Taste," which its website explains "is a living catalog of delicious and distinctive foods facing extinction." SlowFoodUSA remarks on its website that, "The Hog Island fig is notable for the rich complexity of its flavor profile. Fully ripe, it presents itself with an intense floral favor that yields to an earthy sweetness."

The account of Bill Doughty's discovery of fistfuls of Portuguese gold *Johannes* coins and an emerald ring is interesting. Because it is dense, gold commonly sinks deep into sand until it hits something solid—in this case, the loam and clay of the primordial forest below the dunes of Hog Island. There are numerous "money wrecks" and "coin beaches" along the eastern seaboard from Maine to Florida, and the men of the Life Saving Service were alert to the possibility of finding old silver or gold specie at the base of a cut dune or on the surface of exposed marsh mat following storms.

The epic rescue of 26 crewmen from the wreck of the *San Albano* on Hog Island in the middle of a brutal northeast storm is described in the *Annual Report of the Operations of the United States Life-Saving Service for the Fiscal Year Ending June 30, 1892*. Keeper John E. Johnson received a gold medal and bonus from the Treasury Department, his men were honored with silver medals, and the entire crew was issued "a medal of honor and a diploma" from the Spanish government. There was a "James A. Doughty" on the Hog Island crew, but no mention of Bill or Roxalana (or any female crew on the *San Albano*) appears in official records.

As for Hog Island itself, it has been losing ground to the Atlantic Ocean since it was first inhabited. Storm surge from the great hurricane of 1933 submerged the island for a couple of days, prompting residents to abandon the town of Broadwater. Many placed their homes on barges and floated them to the mainland, resettling in the neighborhoods of Oyster and Willis Wharf. They brought clippings from their fig trees with them. Those who spent their childhood on the island could never forget it.

Blackbeard's Burgoo

Every portion of this story is supported by the historical record up to the point it asserts that some mysterious persons have possession of both the transcripts from the 1719 trial of Blackbeard's crew and his silver-lined skull-cap, which disappeared from the Raleigh Tavern at an unknown date. The late Judge Harry Whedbee's account of drinking from Blackbeard's skull with a secret society on Ocracoke Island is found in his charming 1989 book, *Blackbeard's Cup and Stories of the Outer Banks*.

Surf 'n Sky Crabcakes

After this book was first compiled, the State of Maryland and federal wildlife authorities interpreted the Migratory Bird Treaty Act to protect common seagulls as migratory fowl, including those that appear to spend their entire natural lives not migrating at all beyond the four corners of the city dump. So, even if the precise ingredients for Surf 'N Sky crab cakes were known (they are not), they would not be included in this volume because the use of seagull in any dish would constitute a misdemeanor or felony depending upon the temperament and ambition of whatever prosecutor would be assigned the case.

As described, the remarkable career of the James Adams Floating Theater has to be admired as much for seamanship as for anything else. After changing ownership, the Theater sank a couple of times and was refloated, but was finally lost to fire in 1941. It is difficult to overstate the enthusiasm with which the Theater's annual visits were received by the lonely inhabitants of dozens of tiny towns along the Chesapeake Bay.

Edna Ferber spent a very profitable afternoon with Charles and Beulah Hunter in April 1925, taking notes as they recounted their adventures aboard the Floating Theatre—the ensuing novel and play made her wealthy. Ferber was a reporter before she became a novelist, and her ability to spin out a tale from the limited encounters she had with the Hunters and the Theater is to her credit. She once sent Charles Hunter a check by way of thanks, but the amount is not known.

Menhaden Burrito Bombs

This story rightly points out that menhaden are perhaps *the* essential fish in the Chesapeake Bay, serving as a food source for everything from whales to loons, and performing the valuable function of removing nitrogen from Bay waters by eating plankton. Menhaden is very rich in omega-3 fatty acids, and is commonly ingested by humans these days in fish oil supplements.

The flamboyant visionary Brigadier General Billy Mitchell proved to the U.S. Navy on July 21, 1921, that little airplanes could indeed sink a capital ship. He and his men bombed the surrendered German battleship *Ostfriesland* from the air until it finally turned over and sank in the Bay. Mitchell was not flying an S.E.5a at the time (a fighter plane known to occasionally throw a propeller) but a De Havilland DH-4.

Mitchell told a Congressional committee that a "thousand bombardment airplanes can be built and operated for about the price of one battleship." That statement, and his early demonstrations of kinetic air power against anything that floated, made him no friends in the Navy.

The story relates that General Mitchell and some farm workers, apparently of Peruvian origin, dropped ordinance and tear gas on rioting miners during the Mingo War. This is not supported by the historical record. Mitchell was directed to fly some bombers over to West Virginia from Bolling Field as the crisis escalated; he merely suggested to the press that dropping tear gas might be a good idea, but never had the chance to do so as the rioters disbanded.

Lost Boys Oyster Stew

This tale is a paean to the craft of boat-building along the Chesapeake Bay. An excellent contemporary reference on the art is *Small Boat Building*, by H.W. Patterson, first printed in 1943.

The story accurately portrays some of the personalities and events occurring on the western shore in the early 1930s, as well as the growing enthusiasm for small-boat building and racing.

"Overseers of the Poor" like Joe Friedl in the story had a long history in Virginia of caring for penniless individuals and families. In his 2000 article, *The Treatment of the Poor in Antebellum Virginia*, historian James D. Watkinson commented that "the poorhouse and the poor farm surely were lifesavers for many people, especially for the physically and mentally afflicted and the aged poor, whether black or white, free or slave." Overseers were authorized to "bind out" indigent children as apprentices to learn "a reputable trade" as late as 1902. I am unable to determine when the practice formally ended.

There is a large collector's market for oyster cans such as those described in the story. Many are colorful and have beautiful graphics, and are rather expensive to buy.

Ye Corne Hole Cakes

This narrative implies that Sir Arthur Conan Doyle failed to return some rare manuscripts he had borrowed from the British Library, and that he claimed the documents were lost in an explosion on the London Underground on October 30, 1883. That seems improbable. However, it is true that members of the Irish Republican Brotherhood lit off bombs at the Paddington and Westminster Bridge stations on that day during the so-called Fenian dynamite campaign.

While it is very suggestive that the Cornish miners, among them "Sherlocke Holmes," were early practitioners of the "syance of deduction," there is no record of the 1610 affidavit in the British Library and the miners do not appear in any other historical narrative that I can find. So, there is no reason to connect the affidavit with Conan Doyle's fictional character Sherlock Holmes, who portrayed deductive thinking as an "exact science" that "should be treated in [a] cold and unemotional manner" and which the romantic Doctor Watson found nearly impossible to follow.

The story accurately describes Captain John Smith's person and exploits, but the affidavit further muddies the historical record around Smith's dramatic encounter with Powhatan and Pocahontas. Historians look questioningly on Smith's claim that Pocahontas saved his life by throwing herself between Smith and members of her tribe who were about to kill him. The National Park Service comments on its website that, "[w]hether the event actually happened or not has been debated for centuries. One theory posits that what took place was an elaborate adoption ceremony; its adherents believe that Smith's life was never in danger (though, he most likely would not have known that)."

As a military man, Smith was chiefly concerned with the survival of the colony. He bitterly criticized the early colonist's preoccupation with finding gold in Virginia at the expense of readying themselves for the travails of life in the wilderness.

Floater Stew

After the Jeffersons Island Club lost its clubhouse to fire in 1946, it relocated to St. Catherine's Island in the lower Potomac River. It remains a rustic retreat for its members.

In suggesting that people can or should eat "floaters," the speaker in this fragment—who apparently played some role at the Treaty of Versailles after WWI—was likely intoxicated or playing a practical joke in very bad taste.

Bay Hundred Boot Loaf

Hessian soldiers recruited from the Austrian Empire were effective fighters and were referenced in the Declaration of Independence, which charged George III with "transporting large Armies of foreign Mercenaries to compleat the works of death, desolation and tyranny, already begun with circumstances of Cruelty & perfidy scarcely paralleled in the most barbarous ages, and totally unworthy the Head of a civilized nation."

While the British visited Tilghman Island briefly during the Revolutionary War (and apparently later in the War of 1812), there is no evidence that Hessians were stationed there.

The notion that Hessians "baked" bread in their boots after a long day in the field is a fanciful invention, so far as I can tell.

CPSIA information can be obtained
at www.ICGtesting.com
Printed in the USA
BVHW040841280820
587261BV00007BA/156/J